REDSINE NINE · JULY 2002
EDITED BY TRENT JAMIESON AND GARRY NURRISH

REDSINE
a quarterly magazine of dark fantasy & horror

ISBN: 1-894815-02-5

Published by Prime Books, Inc.
P.O. Box 36503, Canton, OH 44735, USA
www.primebooks.net

Redsine editors:
Garry Nurrish, Senior Editor - garry@redsine.com
Trent Jamieson, Fiction Editor - trent@redsine.com
Nick Gevers, Interviewer - nickgevers@redsine.com

REDSINE MAGAZINE
PO Box 1287, Toowong, QLD 4066, Australia
www.redsine.com

CONTENTS

MY VAMPIRES ARE US:
AN INTERVIEW WITH KIM NEWMAN

by NICK GEVERS

INTRODUCTION

Born in 1959, Kim Newman is one of the most audacious and stylish of contemporary British Horror or Dark Fantasy writers. His copious knowledge of the literary and cinematic traditions of the macabre has fuelled a creative oeuvre that, mingling clever pastiche with outrageous invention, reinterprets the cultural past with abandon even as it probes the devious surface of quotidian reality. Newman's books are lucid and humane in powerfully phantasmagoric ways: alluring entertainments, they display a deliberated gaudiness that, even at its most bizarre, vouchsafes deep and curious truths . . .

Among Newman's first books were critical studies and compilations: *Nightmare Movies* (1984), *Ghastly Beyond Belief* (1985, with Neil Gaiman), a celebrated assemblage of Science Fiction's worst prose passages, and *Wild West Movies* (1990). The novels and short stories that followed soon achieved wide popular and critical recognition. Under the name Jack Yeovil, Newman contributed to the gaming tie-in subgenre some of its most notable and groundbreaking titles, such as *Drachenfels* (1989) and *Genevieve Undead* (1993); without alias, he produced the novels *The Night Mayor* (1989), *Bad Dreams* (1990), *Jago* (1991), *The Quorum* (1994), and *Life's Lottery* (1999). His alternate-history Anno Dracula series is particularly noteworthy, the last hundred or more years reimagined as a playground for flamboyant and flawed vampires; the volumes so far published are *Anno Dracula* (1992), *The Bloody Red Baron* (1995), and *Judgment of Tears* (1998, title changed in Britain to *Dracula Cha Cha Cha*), with *Johnny Alucard* to come. Newman's counterfactual facility also shows to great advantage in *Back in the USSA* (1997), a superb story-suite written with his old friend Eugene Byrne. His numerous short stories, antic postmodernism at its best, are collected in *The Original Dr. Shade* (1994), *Famous Monsters* (1995), *Seven Stars* (2000), and *Unforgivable Stories* (2000).

I interviewed Kim Newman by e-mail in February/March 2002.

*

THE INTERVIEW

NG: Your first published books were a history of the post-1968 Horror film genre and a compilation of quotes illustrating how daft SF and Fantasy can be. How did you develop your distinctive critical insight into the speculative genres, at once encyclopaedic and entertaining?

KN: By the usual wide range of viewing and reading. Even when I was doing the obligatory fumbles at writing in my teens, I did as much criticism as fiction and I paid real attention to people like David Thomson, Dave Pirie, Carlos Clarens and Ramsey Campbell (mostly, as it happens, critics who also do fiction), as much for the prose as for the insight. In *Nightmare Movies*, I was not only trying to be comprehensive in an area that had only sketchily been mapped out but trying to find a voice that was above fanzine plot synopsis level but not offputtingly academic. I suppose I still am—in my work as a film critic, I'm a consulting editor for both *Empire* and *Sight & Sound*, trying to be at once populist and informed. As for being encyclopaedic, I certainly know a lot about movies, but so do a lot of other people. I have a broader range of interests than some critics, which means that I tend to go for the overarching perspective rather than the narrow-focus on a single film (like Mark Kermode on *The Exorcist*) or sub-genre (Italian zombie movies or whatever).

NG: Your fiction writing is notable for its intensive allusiveness—some of your works are brilliantly inventive collages of actual events, rewritten historical personages, famous characters from cinema and pop literature. As a corollary to what we were saying just now about your development as a critic, you've long been a prolific practitioner of the critical fiction. Are you a conscious postmodernist?

KN: I feel that my critical work bleeds into the fiction, and vice versa. I suppose I was influenced in the 1970s, when I was at school and university, by Philip Jose Farmer and Nicholas Meyer and others who worked in this area. Later, after I'd started writing, I came across Howard Waldrop. I find this stuff appealing, and I enjoy the reference-spotting aspects of it, though I also understand that it turns a lot of people off. One of the things I've tried to do with the Anno Dracula series is write stories and characters that would still be interesting for people who didn't know where or when a particular person comes from. I've been writing and thinking like this since well before I heard the term "post-modernist" and I do choose to write in other modes from time to time. Then again, when I found out what post-modernism was, I didn't throw up my hands in horror and say I should purge myself of this tendency.

NG: Your work is highly cinematic, vividly visual. How does this filmic inspiration affect the writing of your (prose) fiction? To what extent is writing for you a kind of performing art (bearing in mind your background as a cabaret artiste)?

KN: My cabaret background tends to get exaggerated. I did work in a theatre group in the early 1980s as a performer as much as a writer and did gig around with a comedy band, but it was all very unformed and as much a social circle as an entertainment medium, a long long way from the Perrier Award circuit. I'm not sure I agree that my fiction is that cinematic—I do a lot of interior monologue stuff, which translates badly to film as someone standing there thinking. I'm willing to try different forms of narrative—theatrical, cinematic, comic bookish, cut-up, interactive. But in the end it's all about crawling into the heads of characters. That said, I do write quite a bit of fiction ABOUT performing arts—movies, the theatre, music. It's probably a case of writing what you know about.

NG: Before we get on to some specifics of your work: under your own name and as Jack Yeovil, your writings seem strongly interconnected: characters from one tale can surface in others, timelines overlap, intertextual gestures are copious. Are you, like Michael Moorcock, generating a literary multiverse? If so, does your multiverse have the same sort of underlying moral/philosophical consistency as Moorcock's, or is it more ad hoc?

KN: Yes, though sometimes I try not to. I certainly read Mike Moorcock and am a huge admirer of several strands of his work. It may be that one of his underlying moral/philosophical ideas is that since his multiverse is interconnected, from the most literary to the most pulpy, his readers need to buy and read all his books to keep up with it. I think what he has, and what I aspire to, is not so much consistency as a personality. My various works have various moods. It may be that the eclecticism is a way of covering for a narrow-ish range of affects and themes. It should not be assumed that all my stories take place in the same universe, even a multiple one, but—to state the obvious—they do all come from the same skull. As for the reuse of characters and events, it's something a lot of writers do (though it has complex repercussions in film rights) and which I enjoy as well. Sometimes, it helps just to think that people have lives beyond the segments revealed in particular novels and stories; sometimes, characters get enough tiny appearances to work their way up to a lead role. In that sense, it's more like a repertory theatre than a multiverse. Mike Harrison says somewhere that all his work winds together into an invisible meta-series—my guess is that he's hardly unique in that, though he may be one of the few to recognise it from the outset.

NG: In the franchise books you've written as Jack Yeovil, how central is the gaming format to the structure of each novel? Is it in any way limiting?

KN: The first of the books, *Drachenfels*, spins off from the idea of the companions-on-a-quest adventure, then incorporates the whole idea of role-playing into the idea of restaging an adventure as a theatrical event. Certainly, the story nugget grew out of my ideas about gaming, but that's about it. The other stories and novels go different ways. Every project is limiting somehow, and for-hire gigs like the Jack Yeovil books come with inbuilt agreements about things you do and don't do with a world owned by someone else. In practice, this boils down to simple things like not swearing. My experience with Games Workshop was that they were as happy with expanding the envelope of what was possible in their books as most other publishers. I probably couldn't keep writing Warhammer or Dark Future (the two series I did) forever, but I feel the same about franchises that I have generated myself.

NG: Your first full-dress novel, *The Night Mayor*, set the noir tone of much of your work; yet implicit in the mixture is humour as well. Why, in your view, does the macabre so comfortably incorporate hilarity? To take a recent example, your story "Amerikanski Dead in the Moscow Morgue" (in Al Sarrantonio's 999), a tale of the walking dead, is screamingly funny, a marvellous bureaucratic comedy . . .

KN: I think of myself primarily as a satirist. Most of my stuff does that thing of taking something about the world and exaggerating it to make a point. I've occasionally argued that science fiction is a sub-genre of satire. Of course, satire in the strict sense isn't limited to being funny—horrific exaggeration makes a point almost as power-fully. I like comedy, though, and I like jokes. I doubt I'd ever write a wholly funny book, though I've done some fairly farcical things. Again, a macabre sense of humour doesn't strike me as being uniquely my own attribute. Many of the horror/sf writers I know are very amusing conversationalists.

NG: We come to your metier: Historical Horror. *Jago* illustrated your skill there, but *Anno Dracula* and its sequels brought it into full focus. Why is it so appropriate to ransack the past for horrific props and effects? And why—further—use alternate history to this end?

KN: We have a complex relationship to history, both to the real stuff (personal experience, biographies, etc) and the material medi-ated through fiction. In writing about my times, I find it useful to explore the beginnings of trends we are living with or to find parallels between specific events and periods. I'd argue that most of the alternate history I've done is far more concerned with illuminating what actually happened and is continuing to happen than with credible extrapolations of what might have been if things had happened otherwise. Eugene Byrne, with whom I've collaborated on some AH material, might skew closer to the counterfactual approach where credibility and logic decree the imagined world.

NG: *Anno Dracula* is predicated on a different outcome to Stoker's novel: the Count's victory over his tormentors, his marriage to Queen Victoria, a vampire regime in England. Brian Stableford led the way here with his *The Empire of Fear*, invoking the perfectly reasonable logic that beings as powerful and proselytic as vampires would surely aspire to rule the world openly, not lurk abjectly in crypts. When the figure of The Vampire moves from secrecy into the public light, how does its nature change?

KN: Firstly, the question of whether vampires are supernatural beings or some rationally-explicable variety of creature has to be addressed. I assume if there were a large population of vampires, the supernatural explanation would wither away even if there were no believable alternative. Brian imagined an aristocracy of the long-lived, while I imagined vampires might be as handicapped by their attributes as empowered—considering that 99% of vampires in fiction get killed within the stories they appear in, the immortality of the kind is clearly exaggerated. I also didn't think of vampires as a caste or a cabal who might come to power like a government, simply because I can't see a group of obviously selfish individuals forming anything like a faction (the ratio of Counts to minions is troublingly high) and so the world of *AD* is as much as tangle as our own, only with new players in the game.

NG: *Anno Dracula*'s sequel, *The Bloody Red Baron*, is equally effective in its take on the First World War. Why that war? Because it revealed a human taste for blood worse than any vampire's?

KN: The seed of AD was a single sentence in a thesis I wrote at university on turn-of-the-century apocalyptic fictions, locating Stoker's *Dracula* among those imaginary invader novels of Chesney, Wells and Saki. From that, it was an obvious progression, justified by Stoker's text, to make him a real invader, with political and social ambitions as well as spiritual and sexual ones. I knew from the outset that I would do a book with a WWI setting, since I wanted to get into that "imaginary war" area that so proliferated before 1914 and debate the interaction of these fictions with the events of a real war. Also, as the Royal Guardsmen's "Snoopy vs the Red Baron" song suggested, there was something appealing about the very expression "bloody red baron". My vampires are us, anyway. I suppose the mass carnage of the war put individual bleedings in context.

NG: The third volume, *Judgment of Tears* or *Dracula Cha Cha Cha*, has a suddenly sedate setting: Italy in 1959. What makes the combination of the world of *La Dolce Vita* and vampiric espionage high jinks so extraordinarily effective?

KN: Counterprogramming. Having done WWI, I wanted to go for a more trivial, party-like setting. *The Bloody Red Baron* is a male-skewed book, with planes and adventures and male bonding/feuding, so I wanted to go the other way, and do romance, shopping and clothes. I chose the year because it's when I was born, and I cast around for things from the period that resonated, looking at writers and films of the time. As to its effectiveness, it may be that an Anno Dracula book could be done about any time and place—it's a question of sifting through the associations for the vampirish aspects. Which isn't to say that I'll cover absolutely everything.

NG: You've written various further Anno Dracula novellas, including a particularly brilliant take on Andy Warhol, not to mention a look at Francis Ford Coppola filming a version of *Apocalypse Now* in Transylvania. When are you likely to assemble the next AD book? Will it be the last?

KN: I've got a draft of *Johnny Alucard*, which includes those pieces and some others which have appeared separately or will be original to the novel. It still needs some work, and will probably not show up until I can gather the rights to the whole series and arrange for republication in uniform editions (which has never been done before). It's certainly intended to be the last, for now. Though, as some have complained, none of the books in the series have closed endings—there is no "normality" for this world to revert to, and part of the point is that the continuing characters continue rather than come to neat full stops.

NG: Another potent alternate history is *Back in the USSA*, co-authored by Eugene Byrne. This is elaborate historical inversion—communist USA, capitalist Russia, full of acute ironies of history. How did the concept come together? Chairman Al Capone instead of Stalin, famous serial killers at work on the collective farms, Kurt Vonnegut impersonating Gorbachev . . .

KN: Eugene had a very bad back problem and I had just broken up with a girl. I went to Bristol so we could be miserable together, and it was at the time the Berlin Wall came down. We just started talking through the scenario, which is the frame of the first USSA story, "In the Air", and plotted the novella over a weekend. I was at school with Eugene and we've worked together on and off for twenty-five years, so it was a natural collaboration. I think we didn't really work out the background of the series until the second story, "Ten Days That Shook the World"—there, Eugene did a ton of research and created the history of an American Revolution, and I turned it into ten vignette scenes. After that, we just did stories to fill in gaps in time and geography—covering the Depression, the 1950s, Russia and Britain, each time looking around for a piece to fit the hole. "Citizen Ed", for instance, came about because we needed an American story to fit between the Russian and British ones, a first person narrative taking place over several years, at least a sketch of what happened in WWII and a sense of how Stalinism might value Evil.

NG: Although none of it is so far published, you and Eugene Byrne have worked fairly extensively on a multi-volume alternate history of an Axis victory in World War Two. What's the present status of this project, and where on the Web can details of it be found?

KN: A first chapter of the first novel, *The Matter of Britain*, is up on the

Newman-Byrne website (www.angelfire.com/ak2/newmanbyrne/). The plan is to do six novels, set in successive decades, following the course of a Nazi-occupied Britain through until the break-up of the Thousand Year Reich. Our model is the family saga *Heimat*, and we'll follow a village through the years, though the characters spread out to other locations. *The Matter of Britain*, set in the early 40s, is all about a village in the West Country, but the idea is that the second book, set in the mid-50s, will take place in London during a Nazi-style Olympic Games. As to status, no one has bit for the long term yet but we live in hope that some visionary publisher will show up. We'd like to do it as a huge TV serial, too.

NG: A recent novel, *Life's Lottery*, is quite strikingly innovative. Can you detail the genesis of this book?

KN: Though I was a bit old for the craze, I noticed the "choose your own adventure" books of the early 1980s and thought there might be something interesting in the structure. With Neil Gaiman, I wrote a short humorous version of one of these, published in UK *Penthouse* in about 1984 (good luck finding a copy). It was technically interesting and Neil and I enjoyed the sadistic aspect of tricking the reader into unwise moves that didn't get the avatar any closer to their objective. So, years later, I decided to do a literary novel with the CYOA format. I looked at a few game-books, but other than the idea of numbering and pointing didn't find them that helpful. The choices in most of them seemed limited to practical things like picking a door to open, and I was more interested in moral choices. It was, of course, a tricky book to write (not to mention edit, copy-edit and proofread) and I lived for a year with a chart full of post-it notes and arrows and numbers to keep track of the project.

NG: You've written many short stories, some of them recognised classics: I think of "Ubermensch" (what if the infant Superman had landed in Germany?), "Famous Monsters" (a Wells Martian as a B-movie Hollywood actor), "The Wandering Christian" (a title that speaks for itself), countless others. Which are your favourites? And: are there any further installments forthcoming in the same camp Seventies series as "Tomorrow Town" (on *Sci Fiction*) and "Egyptian

Avenue" (this last in the new Sheehan/Schafer anthology, *Embrace the Mutation*)?

KN: I don't really have favourites among my own works, though there are one or two pieces I like less than average. As with novels, I tend to like the things I've been working on most recently more than the older stuff, but that's more to do with being in a still-thriving relationship rather than feeling a thing is finished and familiar. That 70s series, which I hope isn't camp to the exclusion of everything else, will certainly continue—I've an idea how to bring the characters into the present without going too Austin Powers. I'd also like to continue the 1920s series (which connects with the 1970s things) I began with "Angel Down, Sussex".

NG: In conclusion: what's your estimation of the present general state of Horror (or Dark Fantasy) cinema and literature?

KN: Commercially, books seem to be in limbo but movies are thriving. Artistically, there's good and bad work in the usual proportions. The culture still needs Horror as a genre.

THE ORACLE

by KIM WESTWOOD

In the temple at the end of the world, the Oracle of the Blast is splecked with bronze and gold and oiled by acolytes until slick and shiny. She stands at right angles, hieroglyphic; but every now and then she obliques her head, refolds her limbs into acutes and deigns to speak.

"I will plug in to the universe and talk to you from my third eye," she says, thrusting five digits into a wall socket. Her body tenses, wired for celestial sound, and her eyes roll like dice until only her Cleopatra eye written in blue kohl on her forehead is still looking. The acolytes wait, they sweat, they smell bad. Nothing moves except lice. The Oracle twitches, her eyes open: a pair of aces.

"Oh my darlings," she says to the acolytes, the pilgrims sitting silently at the end of the world, "you have eaten hope out of the apple—and there are no more apples."

The Oracle has spoken. The acolytes file out of the temple below a twisted neon. TOYS "R" US it says.

*

Outside, heat and despair have written on the earth in relentless alternations; volcanic ribbons leach from the temple down Oracle Mountain, slaking its sides raw. Cally stands on a rock sliced from the cliff face above, staring out across barren acidic plains as Mig climbs the scree towards her. Mig clanks; she's been shopping for belts amongst the bodies. She wears several of them across her bare shoulders bandito style and calls up to Cally.

"Lovely weather, eh?"

A seam slithers down Mig's leg as she moves. Mig is more than a bit mad. She cut through her skin to see if it was really like they said: that the kneebone was connected to the thighbone, and so on. A very concrete, visual kind of person as well as mad. Cally had to stitch her up with a sailmaker's needle and a long red bootlace. She thought that Mig would never walk again but Mig had excellent powers of recovery—maybe it was because she never let thinking get in the way of anything.

"Hey," says Cally, "I like your belts; I like the way your nipples can't decide where to poke out."

*

When night spills moon onto the temple, the acolytes are sleeping folded like moths into the smooth hollows they have sculpted within the aura of the Oracle. She sleeps standing, one eye always open, palms turned up to catch inspiration, while outside the neon glows a gentle halo. Only the post-apocalyptic owls are out, sitting on the ribcages of the nameless floating dead and watching for the glint of unclosed eyelids. Moon sets like milkskin on the objects at the end of the world; in a devastation of metal, skeletons stripped of their names angle up to the sky caught halfway between salute and escape. Inside one, its shredded canvas hanging in little tattered rows like prayer flags, Mig and Cally are wallowing in a slow ocean of dream, tucked into each other' s bodies, limbs folded into visceral lychee crescents. Cally is Prince Caspian at the prow of the Dawntreader sailing toward Narnia. Brave and freshly bathed, she sails up onto a land lusciously green, where metal is still shiny with promise. Locked in heroic dream, her captain's hand traces the lightning strike of Mig's leg like it's a map. Mig is dreaming of jet planes and belt buckles and knife handles.

*

On the other side of Oracle Mountain, at the edge of a large crater, there is a feast hanging by wires from a Hills hoist. Henry has threaded each of the eyes of the dead with a hook and is waiting patiently for an owl to beat down between its shadow and the moon and snatch at the dangling treasure. He still has a vivid recollection of a time when dinners did not include owl. The day the sky avalanched down, cracking the earth like a macadamia beneath him, he had been out pegging the washing, intent on matching up the pairs of socks and thinking about meat and three veg on willow pattern plates. For Henry that day was marked, not by culinary loss, nor even the loss of humanity—his town obliterated around him—but by the loss of silence. When his mind shuddered back into his body, his slippers were charred and his house was a deep hole. The Hills hoist was bent over him like a broken umbrella and there were high electric wires singing in his head. As Henry sits waiting for owls, the night sharpens on a thousand metal edges. The dark sings piano wire tight. The stars hurt. More than anything, more than dinner and the return of his neighbours with their neat Saturday suburban green, Henry longs for silence.

*

At sunrise, on the plain below Oracle Mountain, prayer flags are shoved apart.

"Time to go," says Mig buckling belts.

Cally, watching her, remembers the days when Mig was saluted on the tarmac in her air force blues before climbing into a jet and thumbing up the OK. The days when she, Cally, was a ground technician, Aeronautical Division, the smell of avgas always in her nostrils. She watches Mig and remembers life rich with secrecy. Back from the sky, Mig would take her into a corner of the hangar, pull back her overalls and with lips still cool from altitude kiss her nipples until they hurt. Mig, in the crash and burn, had forgotten all that. Her mind, successfully erasing horror, had stripped her memory clean and now she lived only in the present, leaving Cally to hold all the memories that she could no longer contain. Mig's past was etched on her body but only Cally could decipher the scribbles. Daily historian for a landscape set adrift of its past, she watches Mig adjusting belts and ritually repeats the act of remembering. But every now and then, fragments of the past split the surface of Mig's present: more belts than skin, boots like beef jerky stretched and buckled above the knee, she grins at Cally.

"Belt up and live," she announces before climbing out into the morning.

*

Mig's second attempt to see under her skin happens without warning. They are at a munitions dump. While Cally is filling water the colour of verdigris from the nearby bore, Mig is collecting all the white things. As she stands turning a long, bleached bone over and over, Cally catches a look in her eyes but is too slow to understand the question. Mig has already pulled out the hunting knife and is dragging it intently across her skin before Cally moves. When she does, launching at Mig with a cry and taking the knife, Mig looks at her uncomprehendingly, her eyes still full of question.

"But didn't you already find out?" Cally shouts at her. "Why don't you remember the answer for once?" And she hates where it is that Mig has gone. She hates the smooth dangerous skin of Mig's mind. She thinks of living at the end of the world without her and is afraid for herself.

This time Cally has nothing to strap the wound with but some of Mig's belts. Mig is very unhelpful. She laughs at Cally's efforts to stop the blood.

"Come on girlie, put your lips here," she says, pressing her finger to her own.

Cally straightens, Mig's blood sticky on both her hands, and cautiously watches the strong smiling mouth that used to heat-seek in the hollows of her body. The memory twists in her solar plexus and she desperately wants the old order back. She wants to succumb again to Mig's slow deliberate touch, her unerring sense of direction. But Mig does not remember where to go next. She flicks her tongue out at Cally's nose. Laughs. She forgets what she asked and why. Blows like a horse.

"Yum yum yum," she says and walks away.

*

Cally takes Mig to the Oracle as it is clear that she is the only one left with a power point. It takes a whole day to get there because Mig is no longer paying attention, stumbling over her feet and walking into rocks; Cally has to hold her up to keep her from slipping like a piece of loose shale back down the mountain. Beside the old scar on her leg the new cut is bleeding a bright parallel line between the belts. When they pass below the neon, Mig is shaking from the loss of blood and mumbling. Acolytes emerge to sniff the outsiders so lusciously rich with the dirt and sweat of the bright wide plains; they open and close their thin arms like party parasols and usher them into the temple. Cally and Mig are led down long tunnels into the hot shiny heart of the Oracle's home. Mig has stopped mumbling, her breath rasps out of her lungs. The acolytes whisper a sea around them. Their voices shush like waves along the walls. The acolytes can smell the coming of the ritual.

*

Henry has run out of wire for his eyeballs but he knows where there's lots more. He trudges across his crater to the munitions dump where he thinks he is seeing mirages and waits anxiously for them to disappear. He sees the bigger mirage of the two cut into her leg and the little one rush at her shouting. Drawn by the deep vermilion slash that leaves a little trail of droplets like red mercury on the hot stones of the earth, Henry follows them up Oracle Mountain. But as they are shepherded below the neon, Henry is spooked by the flapping of acolytes too reminiscent of owls caught in the wires of his Hills hoist and, fearing retribution, he hides. Left outside, Henry hovers unhappily between the desire to go home and visions of nasty flapping dinner portions bigger than owls.

In the belly of the temple, the Oracle is plugging in. There is something vaguely familiar about her. Cally has the beginnings of a memory, the avgas is again in her nostrils, but gone before any picture comes. The Oracle, still tuning to the heavens, turns her opiate eyes to Mig and sees the angry new snake on her leg. She gestures to her. Mig, mesmerised by the gold flecks dancing on the woman's skin, comes close. The Oracle kneels down at right angles to Mig's thigh and unbuckles the belts then turns her face to the cut and bites. Mig lets out a roar and collapses, Cally rushes to her as the acolytes wave their bodies and sigh like a field of poppies about to be bled. They are in ecstasy. It is a sign. Everything is a sign. Mig does not move and the Oracle's eyes have begun to roll.

"Oh my darling," the Oracle says to Mig before the heavens tighten her in their electronic arms, "one snake is more than enough for you."

*

When Mig and Cally stumble out of the temple, the sky is black and about to burst. Mig's cut, cauterised by the Oracle's electric bite, is already puckered and closing but it is too far to home so they slide down shale slopes to find shelter amongst the boulders rolled to the bottom. Henry follows miserably—it's raining purple and he can still remember that no rain should ever be purple. They crawl into a shallow cave that smells of incense and ashes and has a low wide entrance back into the mountain. Henry sticks his head around the corner, breathes in, and remembers his slippers.

*

Once, every evening, they had rolled obediently to his armchair and waited for his feet. This was because Henry had fitted them with remote control and retractable wheels. An excellent toy maker, Henry worked in a big silver building that sat high on its own bright astroturf hill and reflected the clouds passing. At its entrance swung a candy-coloured neon: TOYS "R" US it said. Inside, Henry worked long hours attending in minute detail to his little machines. TOYS "R" US were very pleased, as his fortuitously Virgo mind made them lots of money—it also earned him the nickname "Microman" among his far less Virgo workmates. A testament to Henry's entirely technical mind was that he never even once wondered if it was a sneaking reference to some of his own body parts.

It was with Sci-fi Barbie that he had struck trouble. Somehow, she managed to develop her own mind along with her intergalactic wardrobe. She talked back at Henry, and when she turned 18 months old, wanted her independence. TOYS "R" US were delighted. Sci-fi

Barbie was destined for great things they said. Henry, miffed, hoped not. He hoped to one day dismantle her and make something more compliant with her parts, but Sci-fi Barbie's superior capacities and extensive wardrobe were delivered to the military instead. When she left, Henry breathed big sighs of relief and said good riddance. With her gone he would have much more bench space; he could make obedient things, like slippers.

*

The rain is sliding down the rocks and pooling like octopus ink where Mig and Cally are lying. Cally is tormented by dreams of the Oracle in an air force uniform strutting along the troop lines inspecting them for lice. She stands in front of Cally and Mig and sees a picture of the other in each of their eyes.

"You two must be disconnected at once," she says and starts to reach out a plastic Barbie hand covered in little blinking electrodes.

Cally wakes up sweating in the grape purple darkness and smells avgas. Mig is lying against her snoring, the cut has opened again and is seeping little flecks of gold. Cally looks into the wide black of the mountain and knows that they have to go back in. When Mig wakes up and Cally tries to explain, Mig doesn't question; she smiles crookedly, slaps her bad leg and says "Tip Top's the one, mum".

Henry, who'd had a very bad night under a nearby rock, follows them hissing annoyance like Gollum after his precious, the memory of his charred slippers stirring yet another memory down deeper.

The passageway is coated in a delicate grey dust that when disturbed, reveals their reflections in dull silver. As they get closer to the temple, they can hear the sycophantic flapping of acolytes and the warm sputter of oil. The corridor ends with a metal door, its security-coded handle hanging from its socket, which gives way when they push. At the far end of the room, on the other side of one-way glass, the Oracle is being painted with sheets of gold leaf dipped in oil from the offering bowls. At her feet the pilgrims are in vigil, their pumice-grey skin flaky as paperbark. Between the door and the glass, banks of mainframe flicker and silent computer screens spool through the flight plans of dead pilots and the schematics of dead aircraft. Cally sees battleships targeting each other and submarines colliding with land as familiar territory slides past and black crosses mark the spot on hometowns. She opens a drawer in a metal filing cabinet to find it full of little slides in plastic sheets and holds one up. The Oracle, resplendent in air force blue, is showering pre-flight blessings from a military balcony. She picks another sheet. The Oracle, dressed in camouflage green stylishly accessorised with an emerald beret, is addressing the ground force troops. In another she is in evening wear, revealing perfectly matching triceps and biceps. Cally stands holding a sheet-full of slides, staring from the Oracle to Mig and back again. Mig is entranced by the screens; they are reminding her of something lovely long ago, the vision of sky turning over and over.

Henry, who has been peering possum-like through the opening, his brain painfully connecting the dots, cries out in an agonising rush of recollection. This is his workshop. Someone has been sitting in furniture, using tools and not putting them back—and he knows who. He can smell her. The whole room reeks of her wilfulness and excess, the flashy fashion accessories that she plastered over herself, rebelliously covering up his precise, painstaking handiwork. The ends of his fingers sting pins and needles and his lips go numb as he realises what else she has done. He launches himself into the room and starts pulling metal cabinets away from walls and crawling around the back of metal casings, scrabbling behind them for the only antidote to all that wilfulness: her precious little interface, her connection to the neon, her power point. Henry finds the plug and pulls. Sci-fi Barbie stops mid-gesture; outside the neon fizzes and spits, and the Oracle Mountain is released into darkness.

*

Sci-fi Barbie had become a terrible success story. Her superior capacities became the eyes and the ears of the military until they thought they no longer needed any of their own. But she knew how important it was that they feel useful, so she kept them busy with increasingly complex diplomatic blunders and false alarms, and planned them tough reconnaissance trips into enemy territory, making sure to lose some of them along the way to ambush and double-cross. It was so much better than silly old chess. When Sci-fi Barbie decided to organise Armageddon, she simply rewrote their computer files, put big fat blips on their radar screens and then sent them all e-mails about it. Staring at the blips, they saw the enemy deploying, and launched into battle. At the same time, Sci-fi Barbie readjusted all their coordinates. Blinded by her all-seeing eye, they flew shiny-buttoned and neatly pressed to bomb their own backyards, all the time thinking that they were above foreign territory, being useful, saving the world. As a grand finale, she lined up all the fighter planes in giant arrowheads along the sky, plotted their course and speared them straight into disaster. It was Sci-fi Barbie who had plunged Mig into her terrible descent and in one hot exhalation taken Cally's brash lover away; Sci-fi Barbie had eaten all the hope out of the apple.

*

There is smoke pluming out of Oracle Mountain. The acolytes have discovered the Oracle's little secret and in their blind flapping rage have wrenched her limbs from her torso. Wires poke out everywhere. "Plug in plug in plug in," she is saying, face down. Bronze and gold splecks are smeared in hot arcs across her thrashing body, oil burns big bright flames toppled from the offering bowls. Amidst Henry's scattered tools and tipped up furniture, LEDs bleed all their colour over broken consoles and computer screens gape big empty holes. The acolytes have remembered themselves back in the air force hangar up and running in their regulation overalls with Sci-fi Barbie's voice booming out to them above the screams of jets. "Patch in patch in patch in," she booms. They up and run to her every command, not because the world is about to end but because they fear Sci-fi Barbie's retribution, her nasty metallic temper. Now the acolytes have seen their past flashing by on-screen and they have smelt avgas. Burnt by memory they have fled the temple, and fluttering injured down the sides of Oracle Mountain, they tumble into crevices and fold like moths back into forgetfulness.

*

But Henry was the real cause of the end of the world. Sci-fi Barbie's irascible maker, in refusing her heart's desire, her dream to become the first cyborg to win Miss Universe, had marked her nascent per-

TOYS'

sonality with a big smudge that spread like a bruise over her cybernetic heart and bent the trajectory of her meteoric adolescence. So, when aiming the fighter pilots at high buildings and submarines at continental shelves she was thinking of Henry, stuck-in-the-mud no-fun Henry, who had spoiled everything by sending her to work for the military instead. He never had the chance to tell Sci-fi Barbie that it wasn't him who sent her there, and that what wanted to do was melt her down and start again. But now Henry is happy. The high electric wires have stopped singing in his head. The stars will no longer scream all night at him from a distance, and when he puts his head down to sleep, there will be only his heartbeat. Deep inside Oracle Mountain, he sits amongst the smouldering clumps of circuitry and skin, secateuring away with his little pliers, humming contentedly. He will neatly sort her into piles and then he will make himself a new pair of slippers.

*

Across the plains, Mig is standing at Henry's Hills hoist, turning the handle. Henry has given her spare wire and the operating instructions but Mig is not interested in owls. The hoist extends like a fun park ride and the eyeballs jiggle on their strings. Mig turns the handle faster and they blur into jet streams until finally the top of the Hills hoist spins off its stand and helicopters into the air before crash-landing several metres away. Mig, delighted, carries it back, shoves it onto its base and starts again. Cally beams. She is sitting on a metal filing cabinet hauled from the heart of Oracle Mountain. Inside are thousands of slides and a little plastic viewer. Soon she will no longer need to contain Mig's past. Mig will start to remember, and Cally will never be alone at the end of the world.

LATE RETURNS

by SHANE M. BROWN

Harry pulled on the handbrake then checked the rear-view mirror to make sure he wasn't being followed. He knew he was being paranoid, but he didn't care; it worked for him.

After waiting ten minutes, looking at the faces in the cars that passed, he grabbed the smooth silver container from the passenger seat and backtracked the hundred meters towards the library. He looked over the cars in the library car park, but couldn't see any that looked familiar. It was unlikely he'd run into any of his work colleagues here, but he couldn't be sure. Libraries were getting popular. He should know.

Holding the book he was returning under one arm, Harry shuffled though his library cards, checked his gas mask was secure, then rushed up the wide stairs. At the top he noticed the library's security system had been upgraded again.

"Damn junkies. They ruin it for everyone," he muttered into his hot mask, appreciating the need for the inelegantly mounted security devices adorning the library's marble columns, but not caring for the way they swivelled to lock on his location. In the last month Harry had read three reports of libraries being robbed. Video stores weren't robbed for their movies. Perhaps the thieves were learning to read. He doubted it.

Swiping his library card through the aperture on the door, Harry turned his face from the cameras and tried to ignore the smell of his mask. Would the librarian be suspicious of him returning so soon? He imagined the data from his card being analysed and added to a database of his library history. At least his returns history was clean. He had never returned a book late. Few could afford a library fine. He had planned to hold out a week before returning to this particular library, but after four days his resolve was broken by mail about the library's latest acquisition. He had phoned ahead to reserve a copy, but it was popular and would only be available on Friday, the librarian had told him. Harry looked around again for anyone that might recognise he was truant from work.

With a familiar hiss of escaping gas that ruffled the material of his trousers, the doors parted for Harry to enter the short decontamination corridor that connected to the library proper. The process was much quicker than at Weir's Public Library on the opposite side of town where it took him almost forty-five minutes before he even saw a book. He heard the smaller libraries were forcing people to make appointments.

He ignored the glass-fronted cupboard that held the library-issue respirators with their milky lenses and stretched elastic. He found the idea of so many people sharing the few masks the library provided disquieting. He never used them, always preferring to bring his own. He wasn't sure if he could even force himself to put one on. He'd stretch his own elastic thank you very much. If you could afford membership, you could afford your own mask. He stepped to one side of the corridor to allow a women and child to pass. It was school holidays, Harry remembered, noticing the pair sported matching respirators, the child's being a scaled down version of her mother's. The woman held to her bosom a metal rectangular container identical to Harry's, while her other arm was occupied with the child. The girl wore a bright yellow dress, with ponytails extending daintily from the back of her mask, like one of those old educational posters Harry had seen from the 1940's when they thought schools might be subjected to gas attacks.

Pushing through the swinging doors to the library proper, Harry scanned the posters advertising the library's latest acquisitions. He had borrowed them all bar one: his day's goal. He read the blurb at the bottom of the new poster: Electrifying, Enrapturing, Unputdownable. It certainly sounded promising. As usual the library was quiet. Most people spent as little time as possible in the library; it was certainly an unwelcoming looking place. He wasn't surprised to see the row of supervised reading booths were empty. In his opinion, the expensive addition of the controversial booths would have been better spent on new acquisitions, or donated to the fight against censorship that Harry had recently found himself an ardent supporter. Feeling the vacuum pulling at his clothes as he rounded the large emergency vents protruding from the ceiling, Harry made his way to the returns counter and stood in line behind a large lady wearing a purple frock with white spots. She was fanning herself with an oriental fan, its yellowed paper, tattered and darkened from sweat, was printed with a geisha standing by a waterfall. There was no way she could feel any breeze from the fan through her mask, although now and again Harry felt the tickle of a breeze on the exposed skin between his mask and shirt collar.

He grimaced at the way the woman held the metal container clamped under her armpit, thankful she wasn't returning the book he was after. Very thankful. After the woman was served, the horrible fan never slowing—let alone being folded and slipped away—Harry stepped forward and slid the metal container across the counter.

From her pleated green skirt and pink top, Harry guessed the library assistant was in her mid-teens, probably working here during the school holidays. She wore a mask unlike any other he had seen. It was made of transparent plastic, but like a funhouse mirror, managed to twist and distort her probably pretty features so that Harry actually reeled back in fright from the glossy projection. The bottom of her mask suddenly flared red, which Harry took a few moments to realise was the mask's interpretation of her red lip-sticked smile. He wouldn't be rushing out to buy one of those, unless overwhelmed with the compulsion to terrify small children. Her mask extended into a firmly fitting transparent apron with full-length protective gloves. He heard the humming of the tiny fans, arranged like gills, which aided air circulation through her mask.

"Didn't you like it?" she asked, running a gloved hand over the container's surface. "It's just that I remember you only borrowed it Monday morning."

Harry froze, although already quite still, and prayed she wouldn't mention this to the librarian. He was sure he was under suspicion at one library; it would take just one phone call for them to catch his system.

"No, it was very good . . . " He ran over the list of responses he had spent the previous evening practising. "I just wanted to swap it for something new." Being the truth, this was not one of the responses. Her hand stopped moving over the container.

Desperate to change the subject, Harry blurted, "That's a new mask you've got on, right? I haven't seen one like it."

The lower half of her mask bloomed red again as she swiped his card and sent the container rocketing through a vacuum tube into the ceiling, supposedly to where returning books were processed.

"I just got it today," she said. "My parents are friends with Mr Higgins, the Librarian. They wanted me to get a job, but I said I wouldn't work here if I had to wear the library's disgusting masks."

"Stretched elastic," said Harry sympathetically. "Milky lenses." He thought he saw the apparition shudder, but it could have been the light.

"Yeah, this one's much better," she said. "People can see my face. Mr Higgins likes that. He says it's good customer service."

From behind him Harry heard someone cough impatiently. He thanked the assistant and left the counter, relieved because the girl's mask was reminding him of the carnival game his parents made him play as a child where you pushed ping-pong balls into a turning clown's head. Every year he had played, the whole time waiting for the clown head to lurch forward and bite his small fingers.

The lending counter was at the library's opposite end, and Harry pressed and held down the buzzer several times to summon the attendant librarian. Behind the long mahogany counter, above the widened doorway leading to the 'Restricted' library area, hung the librarian's many qualifications. The writing was too small to read; they could say anything. They looked a bit faded for Harry's liking, but he was hardly in a position to be choosy. Growing impatient, Harry looked over his shoulder and saw that a man in an expensive suit and matching respirator was slumped asleep in one of the plush armchairs that lined the wall. Definitely not a good sign. A catalogue of books had fallen from his lap. Harry wondered how anyone could manage to fall asleep wearing a respirator, even one of the expensive types with the silicon moulding.

Preparing to hold down the buzzer until the mechanism sizzled to death or someone lent him a book, Harry turned back to see that the librarian had appeared and was waddling towards the counter.

Whoever said you couldn't teach an old dog new tricks hadn't seen this guy. The librarian's body was enclosed within a rigid, protective suit, as if a space suit had been modelled off a lobster. The suit was affixed with an assortment of fragile-looking tools across the man's arms and round torso. Harry marvelled at his ability to avoid tripping on the pipes that extended from his suit back into the restricted section. Although Harry had visited this library more than a dozen times, he had no idea what the librarian looked like, only today learning his name was Higgins. He could have passed the man in the street and not recognised him. The only reason Harry had assumed the librarian was a man was because of the male voice that emanated from the speaker set into the lending desk when the librarian spoke.

"Hello," nodded Harry, feeling a little stupid because they had watched each other for the last minute as the librarian waddled closer. He slid his library card and the notice he had received in the mail across the desk. "I'd like to pick up this book, please." The librarian's entire body twisted as he took Harry's card and ran it several times through a slot in the computer, pivoting between the computer and Harry each time.

"You already have a book," crackled the speaker. "You borrowed it four days ago. Monday, 10.17 am."

Harry glanced over his shoulder to check if anyone was listening. The man was still asleep in the chair, and if anything had slumped down further. Harry wasn't sure if he should address the librarian or the crackling speaker. He decided to lean forward generally and say, "I've just returned it." He pointed towards the returns desk. He wasn't sure why.

The librarian studied him for several moments before retrieving a metallic container from under the counter. On the container was stuck a piece of paper with Harry's name. When Harry reached for it, the librarian wouldn't relinquish his grip.

"Remember," said the librarian, the speaker conveying warning and disapproval. "Only one chapter a day. Some people say that two a day is all right, but trust me as a librarian that knows about these things," he pointed his thumb over his shoulder towards the faded diplomas, or perhaps towards the library's restricted section. "No more than one chapter a day. Less if you can help yourself. Too much work goes into books like these for people to rush through them." Or that is what Harry thought he heard through the static. Assuring the righteous space-lobster that he agreed completely, and that he would pass the message on to the others in his reading circle, Harry took the container and fled the scene, averting his gaze from the carnival clown as he pushed through into the decontamination corridor.

Immediately as he left the library, or the house of horrors as he was becoming inclined to call it, Harry ripped up his mask and inhaled deeply. He hated wearing the mask, but it was a small price to pay. He kept the container on his left side so that passing motorists couldn't see he was carrying a book. It wasn't until he checked in his car's rear-view mirror that he realised that although he had done a good job at hiding the book, it didn't much matter when he was wearing a gas mask on his forehead. He might as well have been carrying the sign, "Just popped into the library. And I've bought my own mask."

He locked all the car doors and rolled up the windows. The last thing he needed was for someone to reach in and steal the book. The replacement costs were ridiculous. He'd checked. For a moment, sitting in the sealed car, he fantasised about opening the container and reading the book right there in his car, in public. Now he was starting to think like a criminal. He'd be arrested for sure. That's what happened to people caught reading in their cars, or any other unregistered place. He'd lose his job. He avoided looking at the container and drove home.

Feeling pleased with himself at having again foiled the library's elaborate security system, he was unprepared to see Brice York's car parked in his driveway. He drove past his house and continued around the block so he would have time to think.

One lap didn't seem long enough, but when his reached his house the second time, Brice was waiting in the driveway.

"Whatever it is, Brice," said Harry, contemplating then changing his mind about leaving the book in the car, "you'll have to excuse me. I'm not feeling well. That's why I'm not at work. I'm surprised you didn't hear." He and Brice shared office space on the ninth floor of the Caruthers Building. In many ways they were in-house competitors. But that meant different things to different people, especially to Brice York.

"That's what I heard, Harry. I dropped around to see if there was anything I could do. I was surprised you weren't home."

"Very thoughtful," said Harry. "But I just need rest. Thanks for dropping around. I'll see you at work on Monday."

Brice smiled with his little mouth and slapped his pockets. "I think I've left my car keys inside."

Harry was out-manoeuvred. His maid, Janice, must have let Brice in. "Have you been here long?" Harry asked as they entered his one-storey brick home, wondering what Brice knew, what he could use.

"I didn't know you had a maid," said Brice, ignoring Harry's question.

"Just Tuesdays and Fridays." Harry looked around his lounge room for where Brice had hidden his keys. They had to be some place where Janice wouldn't have seen them and carried them out to Brice. He would have to explain about Brice York to Janice next Tuesday.

Brice wasn't even pretending to look, just turning on the spot to take in Harry's decor, as if he hadn't just been in the place ten minutes ago.

"What an incredible place," said Brice. "In all the time we've worked together, I've never been in your house. It's like that old television show. The one about the astronaut who has a bottle with a genie inside. What was that show?"

"I Dream of Jeanie," said Harry. That's what people said around the office. Brice knew that.

"That's the show. So how is Michelle?" asked Brice, too casually. "She isn't home?"

"She's fine," said Harry. Michelle had left him weeks ago. He hadn't told anyone from work. He hadn't told anyone. The lingering smell of perfume, something they had argued about, had almost disappeared from their bedroom. Brice had always had eyes for Michelle. He would corner her at parties to compliment her dress, or examine her pendant for an excuse to touch the backs of his fingers against the skin of her throat. At least he pays me compliments, Michelle had said towards the end, and Harry had hated Brice all the more.

"Maybe you keep her hidden in a bottle," said Brice. "I could rub it to make her appear in a puff of smoke."

Harry couldn't see the keys anywhere, but took the opportunity to discreetly slip his library catalogue under a couch cushion.

"I didn't know you went in for that sort of thing," said Brice.

"What sort of thing?" asked Harry, but saw that Brice was looking at the silver container he had brought from the library. This was the last thing he needed. If people found out, they would treat him differently. Like a junkie on the street. And Brice would tell them. He knew it was Brice that had cost Jacobson the Reagent Plaza account, Brice that had squealed to Peterson about Morgan's unauthorised use of the company vehicle, Brice who he had once seen taking notes from the building's after hours log book, looking for patterns he could use to his advantage.

"That's a long way to travel to borrow a book," noted Brice of the container's imprinted logo. "Wouldn't it be easier for you to visit the Weir Library?"

"I would have had to make an appointment at the Weir," Harry explained, wishing Brice would just leave. He'd gathered enough ammunition.

"I'm not sure you should read when you're sick. They're still not sure of the side effects you know."

"I actually have an appointment at the doctors at 2.15," improvised Harry. "I need to get ready. I'll call you a cab."

Brice pulled his car keys from his pocket. "What do you know. They were in my pocket the whole time. You shouldn't be driving when your sick, let me drive you."

"No thanks." Harry showed Brice to the door. "I wouldn't want you to catch anything."

"You know that Stephens lost the Barkley Account. I have reservations for dinner with Roland Barkley tonight. It's a pity you're sick, or you could join us."

"It's a pity," said Harry, shutting the door.

Brice's muffled voice came through the door, "I'll give Michelle your regards, Harry." Or that's what Harry thought he heard.

He reached for the handle but stopped, his hand shaking; he hadn't spent all the effort getting rid of Brice just to invite him back to explain himself. He would deal with Brice after the book.

He took the phone off the hook, locked the doors, then placed the book in the reading room. When sure he couldn't be disturbed, Harry stepped into the spotless shower—he had instructed Janice to pay it special attention—and carefully washed his entire body. He turned the jet of water on full and let it spray long onto his hair and under his arms to remove any trace of shampoo and deodorants. He scrubbed his face and palms with a coarse stone, enjoying the small ritual.

Tearing open the plastic covering of a sterilised towel, he dried himself then hurried naked to his reading room, sealing the door and hearing the vents replace the room's air from its treated supply. The room was distraction free, its soothing colours calming him, and its simple desk and chair were devoid of edges that might cause him injury. Soundproof and airtight, Harry relished the prospect of being undisturbed for the forty-five minutes until the room's automatic safety mechanisms triggered. It annoyed him that he couldn't circumvent the safety mechanisms and use the room for as long as he liked. He hated the feeling of being rushed. He had considered having another reading room installed, but he worried it might draw suspicion. His less desirable second option was to buy his own bookshelf, one with its own air supply that he could wheel between rooms. He had circled one in the catalogue. It was extravagant, but he could afford it. He had little else to spend his money on.

After arranging thick mats around the chair's base, Harry settled and entered his library card number into the container. He exhaled deeply, then suppressing his natural urge to inhale, opened the container and took the large leather-bound book from within. In a much-practised move, without even reading the book's title or author, he opened the first page and inhaled deeply. As far as Harry was concerned, the only important contributor to this book was the librarian. He thrilled at the wave of chemicals that raced from the pages to flood his system, designed to heighten and complement the reading experience by submerging the reader fully in the emotions of the story's characters.

As he had hoped, the first emotion-triggering chemicals that the librarian had infused onto the pages of Chapter One were designed to evoke intense anticipation, unparalleled feelings of expectancy of the type felt only a few times in one's life. But this was only the beginning, and Harry revelled as his anticipation heightened and focussed his senses for the experiences to come.

Keeping his breathing deep and even, and the palms of his hands pressed firmly to the book for tactile absorption, Harry hardly registered the story as his eyes flickered over the sentences and paragraphs, eager to turn the pages and receive the next boost to his artificially induced emotion. For Harry, following the story was secondary to gauging the correct timing of page turning. He had quickly developed his own pace, and far preferred to dispense with the actual story in lieu of concentrating the artificially induced emotions. As he leafed through the first chapter, his anticipation was jarringly replaced with an intense feeling of anger, unexpected as he wasn't following the story. The jarring effect was a warning that he was progressing too fast. He ignored the warning and wallowed in rage. Having dispensed with reading the actual story, his anger was for Brice York. How dare that little bastard come into his house? He'd like to kill Brice York. Strangle the little bastard while everyone at the office watched. He felt like driving over there right now and smashing his car through the front of Brice's house.

Harry fought to control himself from dropping the book and doing just that, realising the book's effects were threatening to cut his experience short. Only through intense concentration did he continued to turn pages, his hands curling into fists and shaking in rage, his face grimacing as he yelled in fury at the desk.

He felt the rage dissipating, and was able to turn the pages faster when, with an electric-like jolt, his rage evaporated and was replaced by fear. If it was possible to describe the overwhelming feelings of dread and terror that had his hands shaking so he could hardly turn the pages, his knees week, his mouth dry, and the hair on the back of his neck standing on end. How could he live without Michelle? Would he ever see her again? He didn't think he could live if she had taken up with Brice. He cried at the thought of them walking hand-in-hand, only now realising how scared he was of being alone. Dying alone.

Turning the pages quickly to pass the terrible emotion, Harry was nearly overcome when instead of the jolt that normally indicated a rushed emotional transition, the next emotion, pure joy, blended with his fear, providing the inhuman experience he craved. Realising this was the point he had failed at so many times before, when his mind forgot where he was and what he was doing, Harry lifted the book to his face and rolled his thumb across the unturned pages. As the last flickering page delivered its load, the book fell from Harry's trembling grasp. He felt his heart thudding in excitement, his stomach churning with nervous butterflies, his bare toes curling in pleasure.

Tears steamed down his face as his mouth grinned inanely. His skin tingled in sensual pleasure where it wasn't covered in goose bumps. His face reddened in embarrassment. In the time it took Harry's body to slump to the floor, he had hosted every synthesised emotion that had passed the censors.

Forty-five minutes later, Harry woke in pain as his head was rocked back as if exposed to smelling salts. The reading room was trying to rouse him. He had a few minutes to respond before it called for an ambulance. The chair had toppled and the mats lay strewn around the room. His left shin was bruised where he had kicked the table leg. He had bitten his tongue and the inside of his mouth.

Harry fixed the room and got dressed, the whole time thinking of Brice's parting words. Had Michelle gone to Brice? Could she be living there? Harry knew Brice's address, had been there for business parties. He would drive there immediately and confront them. Explain to Michelle that he wasn't addicted. Harry found himself pushing the lever to re-cycle the air in his reading room. After he found his car keys, on the way to the door, he placed a freshly sterilised towel in the bathroom. It wasn't until he reached the car that he realised why.

Brice lived on the West Side, right across the road from a public library.

THE HUMIDOR

by L.H. MAYNARD and M.P.N. SIMS

The attic was large and dusty, dirty from the accumulated stale air of many years. It was awash with shifting shadows scuttling away from the hungry beam of the torch, which swung in an arc, dripping milky light over an assortment of boxes, packing cases and old furniture. The shadows skulked away from the fresh clean light, needing the darkness and the cold corners to breed their peculiar dominance.

"There's more than enough up here to furnish the house." Adam Masters said to his wife, who had poked her head and her shoulders into the opening of the attic.

"Do you think we can just take what we want though?" Lauren Masters asked, unsure there was anything in the unfriendly blackness of the attic with which she would feel comfortable. Unsure yet if the newly rented house was something in which she could feel comfortable, uncertain of so much in her life in these recent months.

The torch beam fell with relief onto a light switch on the far wall. Adam picked his way across the rafters and boards and flicked the switch down. A spider-webbed bulb hanging from one of the crossbeam joists flickered into life, grew brighter for a moment then popped and went out.

Lauren instinctively ducked her head away from the sudden enveloping shroud of darkness, and moved down the stepladders into the welcome embrace of the daylight on the landing. "Are you all right?" she called, rather guiltily, as an afterthought. She was very conscious that her husband had been relegated on many occasions to a postscript just lately.

"Just fine. Anyway that's what the estate agent told me, use anything you want."

Lost for a moment, as if the conversation was going on around
and about her but without her conscious involvement, Lauren had a
mental picture of the middle aged estate agent pulling into the drive
of the house in his maroon Rover, and squashing the few forlorn
marigolds that had been brightening up a little flower bed by the
front door. The action seemed to sum up her initial feelings about
the house.

"Are you there? It's awfully dark up here with just the torch for
company."

"Sorry." The man hadn't even noticed the destruction of the flowers, and Lauren wished now she had mentioned it to him. She found
herself wishing she had the courage to actually voice her thoughts
about so many things these days.

"There's plenty of stuff here we can use until we decide what to
do with our furniture in storage."

"You are sure we can use it?" She realised that she was trying to
throw doubt into the conversation in the hope that the answer would
come back that no, they couldn't use the furniture, and in fact they
couldn't have the house. They would have to move back; back to the
bland safety they had just left. Back to the city where her circle of
friends shielded her from the necessity to spend as much time with
her husband as she feared would now be imposed upon her.

"He said we can bring anything down from the attic we want, so
long as we keep it in the house or the garden. Let's face it; we're going
to need quite a lot of it in a house this size. The bits and pieces we've
got will soon be swallowed up."

Lauren had a sudden feeling that it was she who was being swallowed by this house. Not the furniture, not her confident, loveable,
unimaginative husband, but her, Lauren Masters. Swallowed by this
huge dark old house, where the last owner had killed himself.

Adam Masters was still exploring, but as he shone the torch at a
far dark corner of the attic, he failed to notice how the light faded
and misted away at the edges. The shadows in the darkness seemed
frightened of themselves, scuttling away as soon as the torchlight
threatened to bring them into focus.

"Lauren, you couldn't get another light bulb for me could you?

And perhaps a duster and some cleanser."

Lauren made a rare joke about what his last servant died of, but in truth she was glad to get away from the oppressive attic. The opening, with its square of blackness, was like a mouth gaping open in anticipation of its next meal.

She left Adam and ran down the stairs to the ground floor. The house was large, too large for the two of them alone. The early marriage thoughts, hopes even, of children had come to nothing. Now the subject, like so many others between them, was avoided. They had long ago ceased to converse in any close way, it seeming sufficient to pass the time of day, like train carriage strangers. She knew, perhaps he did as well, that it couldn't last like this, but to raise the subject was to indulge in too intimate a discussion than they involved themselves in any more.

Reluctant to hurry back to the beckoning maw of the attic she stopped in the dining room and looked at the work she had started on her easel. A freelance illustrator of children's books she was independent enough in her own right to have resisted the move of house because of Adam's job re-location. Yet she had put up only a token resistance, as if to do any more was to offer more of her than she wanted to share with him.

The charcoal sketch was supposed to be the outline of a family of rabbits, highly stylised but rabbits nonetheless. What she found herself looking at on the board was a muddle of shadows; a sneering countenance of a shadowy figure predominant amongst a host of indistinct shadows surrounding it. Where had that come from? she asked herself. She knew she had been tired when she started the sketch, but surely she would have remembered drawing something like this. Something that was so *sinister.*

Leaving the drawing without wishing to touch it she went into the kitchen where she knew the odds and ends like spare light bulbs were located. She gathered her resolve around her to rejoin Adam.

Adam was waiting at the top of the ladders, tapping the torch against his teeth. Lauren climbed up and handed him the bulb. The darkness was closing in on her again, making Lauren feel uneasy, unwelcome.

Adam fitted the bulb, and switched it on. The black attic became grey with the light, shadows and shapes formed behind the various contents. Old furniture threw distorted images away into the corners; packing cases and boxes held onto the darkness with their mass, like sponges soaking up water. Adam pulled himself up into the attic and Lauren rested her elbows on the chipped wood of the opening. With the attic more wholly lit she could see the extent of the clutter up there.

"What's this?" Adam said.

As Lauren glanced in his direction she thought she saw his shadow move back into position. It was as if it had been moving independently of him and now, with the attention and glare of the light, it shifted back where it should have been. Then, as if that hadn't spooked her enough, Adam seemed to darken. His body became a transfer, as if she was staring at his shadow rather than his body. Then he knelt down to look at something, and the illusion disappeared.

In an attempt to break the tension that was threatening to envelop her she struggled to engage in interested conversation about what Adam was doing. "What have you got?" He was holding what seemed to be a dirty wooden box.

"It's a humidor. A box for storing cigars." Adam surprised himself with his answer. He had no idea what he had found and yet the answer popped into his head as though he was familiar with the heavy object. It was heavy as well. The box was made of solid wood and resisted his initial attempts to open it.

Lauren shrugged. "Not a lot of use to you then." Her husband had never smoked in his life so far as she knew.

"I don't know. I've always wanted to try a really good cigar. I'll take this down and clean it up."

Lauren was almost relieved that they might be able to shut the attic and go back down stairs. She couldn't prevent a note of disagreement though. "What about some furniture? That's what we came up here for."

Adam seemed distracted when he replied. "Plenty of time for that."

Next morning Adam was up early, washed and dressed in his business suit. He hadn't been keen to leave the area they had been born in either, but once they found the house and paid the advance rent, he was happier. Adam kissed Lauren goodbye and got into his car for the ten-mile drive to the new office building. Lauren wanted to spend the day drawing.

The shadows she had consigned to the bin and had managed three rabbit scenes before midday when she became aware of the smell. Her father had smoked cigars, as well as a pipe, so she knew what the aroma was but what she didn't know was why it should be in her house.

The kettle suddenly boiled, at the same time as the easel in the dining room collapsed. Chiding herself for being so jumpy she went through to the sitting room from where the cigar smell seemed to be emanating.

Adam had assigned the whole of the previous evening to a loving examination of the box. Declaring it to be mahogany, he had announced that the heavy lid was a sign of its careful construction. The lid closed tightly, which somehow he knew was important. There was a hygrometer in the inside of the lid, which he lectured her was there to monitor the humidity level. Unvarnished inside, it had trays at various levels, which he knew was "to store different size cigars separately, and to rotate them within the box." When she asked how he knew so much about something that he had never seen an example of before he became quite angry, belligerent even. They had one of their familiar aggressive arguments, and Lauren flounced off to bed.

Now the smell of a burning cigar was prominent in the room. There was no sign of smoke, just the aroma. She searched around the room, but knew she wouldn't find anything. She knew it would be the box that was the centre of the smell.

That evening Adam was home late, tired from a first day in a new job. He was distant, sharing little of the actions of his day with Lauren. She responded by being short with him, replying when he did speak to her, with sharp one-word answers.

"That box of yours smells." She tried a direct approach.

He hesitated for a moment, the fork full of food hovering just outside his lips. "Am I supposed to ask smells of what?"

"Cigars of course."

"That's hardly surprising."

She scraped the remains of her meal into the bin; little caring he hadn't finished. "It is if it's empty, and if it hasn't been used for years."

The night before she had found it amusing to see his disappointment that there were no cigars in it, after he had been eulogising over the dusty box. She had never believed there would be, but clearly he had. The box itself, although well made, even she could concede that, was in need of a long polish.

When they had both cleared away in the kitchen Adam went through to the sitting room and his new toy. Lauren wandered into the dining room and her drawings.

Adam always experienced a little guilt at the relief he felt when he left a room that Lauren was still in. There were problems in the marriage he was well aware, but he truly believed the move and the new start would help. He had long ago ceased to consider whether they still loved one another. To have stayed together for twelve years was celebration of sorts. It was just a rough patch that couples went through. He could almost convince himself, but not enough to try convincing Lauren.

He was surprised when he picked up the humidor. It had been freshly polished, with beeswax by the look and smell of it. A proper job, not a quick flick with a duster. It could only have been Lauren who had done it; perhaps that was why she had brought his attention to it over the meal. She sounded waspish but that might have been her way of telling him she had done it for him, a gesture of some kind.

Idly he lifted the heavy lid, aware that there was a delightful smell surrounding the box. The interior was full of cigars. Various sizes, from the heavy ring gauge to the slender, the gran corona to the entreacto, different colours, the pale brown of the claro, to the black oscuro, a richness of aroma. He picked one out. The paper band said Macanudo, and he immediately knew, though he had never before heard of it, that this was founded in Jamaica in the 1860's and was now made using Connecticut Shade wrapper, binder from the San Andres area of Mexico, and a mixture of Jamaican, Mexican and Dominican tobacco for the filler.

All at once he experienced the sensation of burning within his lungs. The smell of the cigars in the box, and the one in his hand, remained mild, yet he fought to control his coughing, as his chest seemed on fire. He was vaguely aware that the other chairs in the room were all occupied, as though a group of people were around him, watching him. He could see their heads encased in a sheath of smoke, a haze of blue and grey that floated up to the ceiling. As the cigar smoke drifted upwards he could see the figures begin to shimmer and wave, like clouds upon a wind. The smoke grew darker, became shadows, as the figures lifted towards then melted into the ceiling.

He must have cried out because the next thing he knew Lauren was in the room with him. He pointed up to the ceiling and they could both clearly see a large scorch mark on the white paint.

"What the hell are you doing smoking that thing?"

Adam was taken aback to find that he was holding a cigar in his hand, a half smoked cigar.

"Where did you buy it? Why? You don't smoke."

He tried to explain that he had found it in the humidor but of course she had seen it empty the previous night. But then so had he.

Lauren had long gone to bed, in yet another foul mood when Adam decided it was safe to join her. They had not yet capitulated to separate beds, though they just as well might. He was glad these days when he came up and found her already asleep, although once he had seen her eyes open when she thought he wasn't looking.

He had smoked a second smaller cigar before locking up for the night. The humidor he had put in the front porch to keep the temperature reasonable.

Lauren was on her back on the bed, the covers partly dishevelled. She seemed, in the gloom of the dimly lit bedroom, to be sprawled out across both sides of the bed. Then Adam saw movement on one side of the bed while Lauren visibly hadn't moved. It wasn't just her body sprawled across the whole bed; there seemed to be someone else next to her.

At first he had the thought that she had taken a lover and was sleeping next to him, satisfied and spent, flaunting her infidelity as a taunt. That this was ridiculous he immediately realised, and he was torn then in his emotions. His decency wanted him to protect his wife from whatever intruder was lying next to her, but his self-preservation was afraid for himself.

He slowly moved towards the bed. He tried not to breathe, then to breathe quietly and with care. He took hold of the edge of the covers, and swiftly pulled it off the bed. Only when the covers were gone could he see, in what light the moon afforded, that there was someone else on the bed with Lauren.

"What are you . . . " Lauren was now half awake.

The shadow figure slipped off the bed and smoothed itself into one corner of the softly furnished room. Adam wanted to turn on the light but was frightened to move. He was sure he saw the shadow scurrying beneath the bed, but he could even now convince himself that the shadow was just that, a shadow. The moon was hiding and seeking behind the clouds, and the room was dancing with unnatural rhythms. How could he be sure what he was seeing?

Then he saw a black shape take up its position at the bottom of the bed. As Lauren demanded that he turn on the light and stop being so stupid, the shadow at the foot of the bed sloped forward and covered her like an eiderdown, but one that soaked into her body until it disappeared, and Lauren swelled slightly from within.

Adam turned on the light and Lauren was asleep on the bed, the covers neatly over her, like atonement.

Lauren was alone again the next morning after Adam had gone to work. He hadn't wanted to mention the night to her, or to admit anything to himself. She worked through until noon, and then gave herself a break. She lay down with a book in the sitting room.

It was a clear crisp afternoon. Sunlight broke in through the yellowing net curtains, lending a relaxed mood to the room which Lauren found hard to share. She began to shift on the sofa to see if she was alone in the room. As she read a page she looked around her before turning to the next as if she was nervous of making the movement. She felt as though she was in a library and others around her would chastise her for making a sound. The clock on the mantelpiece struck the half-hour and she jerked forward in her seat, surprised by the sudden intrusion of noise. The rustle of the pages of the book began to sound magnified, loud and insistent, like a shout at midnight.

She wasn't sure when she first noticed the change in the room. One moment she was feeling strangely attuned to every sound and movement in it, and the next she was frozen, helpless to respond.

The light playing against the window began to fade until there were shadows in every corner. Furniture became hidden in dark masses of unlit space. Flickers of moving light showered on the wall in front of her, but the innocent shapes and patterns took on a sinister tone that she could not quite discern. Faces appeared on the wall, faces of crying women, and some men; faces of open-mouthed terror calling out for help that the eyes admitted would never come. Faces from which beauty gradually slipped away to be replaced by mean cunning, crueller for the quality of purity it had displaced. Faces that gradually faded into shadow.

Motionless on the sofa she became aware of whispered movement behind her. She tried to turn her head but could only move her eyes. She was dimly conscious of what sounded like black swishing robes, and of someone pacing the floor behind her, and of the light frenzied steps of others. In the reflection of the window in the half gloom, she could vaguely see several figures. A tall corpse-thin figure in robes lighting a thick black candle, a woman kneeling in front of him; oil was placed upon her forehead, it glistened in the muted glare of the candle. She was naked. There was low chanting from different voices; small high voices, and other deep bass voices. Behind them other figures, frightened, excited, passively acquiescent.

Then violent movement overtook the figures as a huge shadowed shape emerged from the blackness at the edge of the room. Wings with claws enveloped the tall thin man, wrapping around him in a fond embrace. A tongue darted from the creature's formless mouth and curled serpent-like around the neck of the man. The others moved silently away, and a wooden box was offered to the creature, and lifted into the air, as if for sacrifice. The tall figure was engulfed so that he struggled and choked. As he slowly died, the beast fed from the man, whose face took on a beatific glow of pleasure.

Lauren's book fell from her numb fingers and the room returned to normal. She could barely remember what she had seen, or was it dreamed? Except she could recall the proffered box, it was Adam's humidor.

When he came home that evening she had cooked a special meal. She was dressed in her best dress, low cut and clinging. The humidor was in pride of place in the centre of the dining table. Its soft aroma of fine cigar smoke was offset by Lauren's subtle scent.

The food was wonderful and the wine was copious. Adam, despite his reservations about possible motive, eventually relaxed into the atmosphere of the occasion and in his inebriated state began to hope that there was a chance of salvation for the marriage. Lauren drank little but cloaked it cleverly so that Adam wasn't aware.

When the meal was eaten and the coffee served Lauren moved behind him and leaned into him, her breasts easing into his shoulder. She held a Saint Luis Rey, the wrapper very dark, smooth and oily, the end already cut in readiness. Slowly, Adam deluded himself that it was *seductively*, she lit it for him.

The humidor was open on the table, the aroma of the passive cigars within a counter balance to the ongoing one Adam was enjoying. There were candles on the table, adding to the illusion of friendly intimacy that Lauren had created.

She picked up a candle and lit the sheaf of paper she had prepared when setting the table. The flames flickered into the air and then she plunged them into the humidor. The loosely packed cigars began to smoulder, the box itself to blacken.

"What are you doing?" Adam struggled to get up from his chair but his legs were reluctant. He had drunk so much, and she so little.

Then they both became aware of the movement in the corners of the room. One of the cigars had ignited and a thick pillar of smoke was rising to the ceiling. The room seemed to be active, and yet Adam couldn't see anyone or anything. Nothing that stayed still long enough for him to see it anyway.

A sound like liquid flesh squeezing and pulling made Lauren look upwards. From the ceiling indistinct shadows were erupting above her head and dropping like rain. Globules of darkness forced their way out through the plaster until they were in the open, and then as they floated down they coalesced into shapes that were nearly human.

Adam was standing now, the smoke from his still lit cigar billowing around his head, a kind of ectoplasm. The cigar smoke seemed to be beckoning the shadows to the room. The humidor on the table was slammed shut, the burning contents ignored.

Lauren started to laugh. Then a large shadow fell upon her from behind and she was pulled to the floor. In the increasing blackness Adam thought he could see a black robed form lying motionless on the floor besides Lauren, holding her. Candles flickered around them, and quiet, frightened figures tried to hide in the shadows. The robed form had the shape of a man but was no longer a man. There was no face, just ruffles of hanging white skin, crinkled like paper, no eyes, and no mouth. The black robes hung deformed from the shrivelled body, wasted, lifeless. The figure was like a cloud of smoke formed into a man-creature, a withered husk on the brink of death.

Adam felt pressure around his neck, as cold claws clamped into his skin. Talon fingers gripped the flesh, cutting deep, drawing out blood. He swung and turned to try to prise the fingers from him, and as he turned he saw what was attached leechlike to his neck. It was large, folded wings hanging to the ground, misshapen horns protruding from the head. The skeletal arms wrapped around Adam were covered in coarse black hair that had worn away in places, to reveal dark, paper-thin skin.

As Adam struggled against the creature he began to feel weaker, and the shadows reflected his weakness. And as the beast was draining Adam's life from him so the figure on the ground was stirring into new life, the black robes filling and swelling as Adam drifted into the darkness. All the time Lauren, lay quietly, conscious but her mind switched off from the horror she had engineered.

The choice was easy to make for Adam. "Take her," he whispered.

The room immediately cleared and the shadows dispersed. There was no sign of Lauren.

Adam thought he might feel some regret in the morning. For now he opened the humidor, pristine inside, and selected another cigar to enjoy.

CLOWNING AROUND

by RICHARD ROBBINS

Loopy's eyes open and he looks around the big top. The tent is empty, the crowd gone, the trapeze still. A pungent pile of elephant dung decorates the centre ring. A giant calliope fills the empty space with music and then stops. He scratches the orange hair on the edge of his bald pate, looks around and sees a roustabout leaning on his mop and smoking a cigarette. Loopy turns around and trips on his size twenty-nine shoes, does a pratfall, toots a brass horn with a red bulb, jumps to his feet and takes a bow. The roustabout puts the cigarette in his mouth and claps his hands, turns around and disappears through a tent-flap. Loopy smiles. He loves to make people happy.

Loopy flip-flops toward the rim of the centre ring, unsuccessfully trying to avoid the elephant dung, which is twice the size it was the last time he looked. He takes fifteen or twenty steps and hasn't moved at all. He tilts his head to the right, puzzled. His porkpie hat falls off its precarious perch and lands on the dung. His clown-smile frowns as he watches the hat roll down the pile. He pulls up his pants, doing his customary little clown dance. As he bends over to pick up the hat, he feels a kick from behind and falls head over heels into the pile. Laughter bursts from nowhere as he sits up. Carefully, he stands, puts the hat back on his head. A thunder of applause explodes from the empty grandstand and then stops. The work lights in the big top go out and the tent is silent. He stands in darkness for a moment. "Hey! What's going on?" he shouts. This can't be real, he thinks. The show's over. The rubes are all gone home to their comfy little houses.

The sound of a relay closing cracks through the silence and Loopy is pinned to the ground like a collector's bug by the huge klieg light snapping on overhead. Loopy's neck hair stands erect in defiance. His mouth dries in anticipation. His white makeup fluoresces blue in the hot glare of the spotlight. He stands alone in the island of light. He takes a step to the right, the island of light moves with him. He runs, trips over his checkerboard pants and does a dive-roll, but the follow-spot anticipates him. He stands, catches his breath.

A second shaft of light opens a bright spot in the centre ring. A Ringmaster appears, striking a pose. The sequins on his top hat reflect bright colours onto Loopy's face. "Ringmaster, what's going on?" Loopy's voice trembles.

Ringmaster points a white-gloved hand at him and laughs. "You will address me as Mr Ringmaster, if you please."

A third light opens to his right, revealing an old dilapidated grey and green clown with an electric nose. He bows and says, "I'm Dimmy." He makes a rude gesture, turns his back and drops his pants.

Another light flashes on and frames a giant red, green and yellow clown wearing a gingham dress, and riding a miniature fire engine in tight circles. "I'm Kibble," he says and bangs his snare drum and tips his flowered hat.

Ringmaster says, "Quiet, everyone. The Clown Court will come to order."

A gigantic desk falls from the very top of the big top. It smashes to the floor, sawdust flies into the air. The spotlights coalesce, casting black shadows over Ringmaster, who takes his seat behind the remains of the desk. Kibble and Dimmy stand to either side of Ringmaster. Loopy stands in front of the desk, his clown face sweating, the grease paint running in great multicolour tears.

"Mr Kibble, will you act for the prosecution?"

"Yes, Your Honour," says Kibble. "It will be my pleasure." He turns a somersault and then manages to stand still.

"Mr Dimmy, will you act for the defence?"

"Aw," answers Dimmy. "Do I have to?"

"Yes, Mr Dimmy," says Ringmaster. "Everyone is entitled to a defence."

"Oh, all right," Dimmy says. He makes a loud blurping noise.

"Fine, let's come to order." Ringmaster hammers the top of the table with a large red rubber mallet. It bounces back and hits his nose with a thunk.

"Why am I here?" Loopy asks. "Where am I?" He takes off his hat and holds it in front of him.

"The prisoner will remain silent!" Ringmaster, Dimmy and Kibble scream, all at the same time.

"Do you waive the reading of the charges, Mr Dimmy?" asks Ringmaster.

"Yes—"

"No, I do not," says Loopy.

Dimmy runs over to Loopy and sprays him in the face with a seltzer bottle. Loopy tries to retaliate, but finds that he's tethered to the ground and can't move.

"Excuse me, Mr Ringmaster," says Kibble. "I don't know the charges and I'm the prosecutor."

"Mr Loopy," says Ringmaster. He punctuates his words with his rubber mallet, careful of the rebound. "You are charged under Codicil CCC of the Clown Code, which states, in part—"

He is interrupted as Kibble sneaks up behind Dimmy and trips him. Dimmy falls to the floor, but bounces up and sprays Kibble with the seltzer bottle.

"Gentlemen, please maintain your decorum," says Ringmaster. "If I may continue?"

"Please," says Loopy. Loopy is feeling increasingly nauseated and starts to retch. He manages to hold it back.

"Which states, in part, and I quote, 'A clown shall not be a meany or a scary person.'"

"I object," Kibble says.

"I join Mr Kibble in his objection, Your Honour," says Dimmy.

"On what basis?" The Ringmaster pounds his gavel.

"I don't know," Kibble answers.

"Neither do I," says Dimmy. "But this is great." He turns a cartwheel and lands on the elephant dung.

"Then be quiet." Ringmaster looks at Loopy with fire in his eyes. "How do you plead, Mr Loopy?"

"I am not mean, Mr Ringmaster," Loopy pleads. "And I am not scary. However, I will admit to becoming very angry with you people. What gives you the right to—"

"Plea is not acceptable. You must plead guilty so we can get on with sentencing." Ringmaster stands.

"Right," says Dimmy.

"You are the defence, Mr Dimmy."

"Sorry, Mr Ringmaster."

Kibble produces a cream pie from under his green and red striped coat and throws it at Dimmy. Dimmy ducks deftly, avoiding the missile, which hits Ringmaster in the face.

Loopy is incredulous. He pulls himself up to his full height, which seems to be taller than he's ever been before, and toots his brass horn. "I am really angry!" His clown-face is running, the grease paint smears his clown-smile into a grimace. "What is this place?"

"The defendant will be seated," orders the Ringmaster.

Kibble asks for an adjournment.

Dimmy objects.

Loopy feels a strange tingling in his mouth. He reaches up and finds two large teeth that were never there before. He looks down at Ringmaster and Kibble and Dimmy. They look up at him. Ringmaster shakes his fist. Kibble bangs his drum. Dimmy falls down. Loopy watches them become smaller and smaller as he grows. He shouts, "I am not scary!" He stamps with giant steps around the centre ring, elephant dung and sawdust filling the air. Suddenly, without warning, his head hits the top of the tent. He barely notices Ringmaster, Kibble and Dimmy as his twenty-foot long shoe crushes them.

His head pushes through the big top, which lies like a giant poncho around his shoulders. He flings it from him and walks deliberately toward the lights from the town in the valley. He catches an aeroplane in his pork-pie hat and puts it back on his head where he feels it buzz. He imagines what the people in town will think when they see a hundred-foot Loopy with orange hair surrounding a bald pate and a pork-pie hat, wearing checkerboard pants. He laughs a terrible toothy laugh as he crushes an entire farm.

I guess they were right, I'm a scary clown after all, he thinks. He toots his mighty brass horn with the red bulb. He stops for a moment and shouts to the world, "It's really fun being scary." His words echo from the mountains. "I think I'll take a walk," he adds, smiling a big clown smile.

Loopy steps over the mountains and walks across the world.

DON'T DROWN THE MAN WHO TAUGHT YOU TO SWIM

by D.F. LEWIS and DAVID MATHEW

"It's about someone who discovers the secrets of the universe as he's drowning."

Nathaniel looked up. "What is?"

"The story I'm writing," said Paul with a pinched expression on his face. "You could pay attention you know, Nat, it wouldn't hurt you."

"Sorry. I just can't make these figures balance."

"Then leave them unbalanced—like the rest of us," Paul replied. He honestly believed that he was being witty. "Do you want some squash?"

"Yes, please. And put some vodka in it while you're there."

Paul couldn't resist a crack as he left the room. "Yes, you're always better at eyeing up figures when you've had a few drinks, aren't you, dear.'

Go to hell, thought Nathaniel. What had he missed? He returned his attention to the towering totals on the sheets of paper before him. Talk about drowning by numbers! He'd be having a word with a few of the team on Monday, that was for sure. Look at that! Bloody Katie: her expenses were always good for an extra few notches up the blood pressure pole, but putting flowers on her claims now, was she? No way. No way, Jose. What did they think he was, some kind of drip?

"Here." Paul laid down a glass, which did drip . . .

"For crying out loud, Paul, not on my papers!" Nathaniel transferred the glass on to a homestore catalogue, but when he wiped at the ring of moisture on the training cost breakdowns for the Marketing Department, the numbers merged and ran like mascara.

"Look at that! Just look at what you've done!"

"You did it!" Paul argued. And then, more hysterically: 'You did it!'

"Just leave me alone, Paul. Go 'way, right now. Right now."

"You can still read it."

With a cavernous breath Nathaniel controlled his temper. "Did I explain to you, Paul," he said, "just how important these figures are? I have here the entire financial autopsy for my silly little company for the current financial year. Are you with me so far?"

"Don't patronise me, Nat."

"Please listen. There are no copies because Acquisitions decided, in its wisdom, to buy a tinkertoy German model of copier, and we're waiting for the engineer to fix it. Again."

Life was usually full of copies, but at the moment he didn't even have an ancient xerox or bakelite gestetner, let alone a dark scanner.

Paul had decided once more to plead for reason. "But you can still read everything," he said, with an angular whine to his voice . . . which Nathaniel could all but ignore these days.

"And this is an auditable document," Nat said. "Believe me, an inspector loves this sort of incompetence. Inspectors love giving companies like mine a kick in the shins."

Now that reason had been proven dysfunctional, Paul would resort to spiky self-defence. He said, "You're just being *melo*." This was his abbreviation for melodramatic. And once he had made this announcement he left the room.

Nathaniel cradled his head in his hands. Hair's thinner, he noted and he sighed. Correcting fluid needed thinner. Just as life these days lacked a splash of toner.

Pages rippled. By now the burning sensation that leaked across his abdomen when he was stressed was in full flow. I am falling to pieces, he thought. Numbers were bleeding in the whites of his eyes, like floaters. He sighed again.

What was it that Iraqi leader had said? Something like: "They will drown in their own blood."

Mid-evening. I still have a few hours, thought Nat. I'll have a bath.

Calm down.

So deciding, he all but winched his bodyweight up the stairs on legs that had no strength. In the bathroom, Paul was admiring his dental work in the mirror. They shuffled in the poky room without a word being exchanged. Nathaniel drew the bath. Firmly wedged in the heat and the plastic a few minutes later, Nat was nodding off and was surprised to hear a knock at the door. Paul had brought him his drink as a peace offering. Paul leaned over and kissed Nat's bald spot. The place where he was at his most vulnerable; a wafer between him and God.

Nat fell asleep dreaming of numbers that scuttled about the table like insects.

Gravity wanted his bones. Over the course of ten minutes, Nat slid down the soap-lacquered side of the bathtub, and the water licked at his chin. Let me in! Water entered his ears with a pop and a suck, and Nat coasted an inch or two deeper. Unguented water lapped around his lips; they were a puddle. Nat opened his mouth, and swallowed.

He was dreaming of a star. A star that would look in-place on top of a Christmas tree, but it was embedded into the cushion of the night, slightly wonky. It looked like a drunken king's crown. The star flapped its prongs like an undersea life-form. It was encrusted and barnacled . . . and it was singing to Nat.

Straining to hear the words made Nat twitch his head to one side. Water leaked against his tonsils. He coughed. I'm drowning, he thought - but the realisation brought no sense of panic. No sense of anything at all. Nat was drowning . . . but he couldn't drag himself away from the star. It was singing the secrets of the universe, but for Nat it was like someone was whispering through a gale. And he wanted to learn.

He came awake with the suddenness of a window blind snapping.

Disappointment rang in his ears as he coughed up his lungs.

Mid-evening had become midnight—and Nat escaped the bath, with some post-suicidal reluctance, noting that Paul had not sloped in to see if he was all right. Very soon he was slug-a-bed, and Paul—who had been feigning sleep—leaned across and kissed Nat's bald carapace. Kissed his baby's cap.

The next morning Paul was up and at 'em early—it was an unusually early start for fiction writers, at any rate. Ordinarily he would wait until Nat had brushed himself down and left for work; Paul liked to believe that creativity was only waiting for mid-afternoon to flourish. Yet Paul was off today at the crack of doom, it seemed. His story still needed a hero, after all.

"What was that story of yours called?" Nat's words from the bed yawned in the face of a half-waking conversation, yet somehow he pretended that he was socialising after a good dinner and a basinful of wine . . . or even a bathful of it. He felt rotten to the core, having recently watched his past life fleet before his mind's eye on that brink of soggy suffocation, a suffocation that his fitful ablutions would ever now bring forth once more. He was usually up much earlier than this for work, and even at the weekend.

"My story called? Well, it hasn't got a title yet. Any suggestions?"

"The only thing I can suggest right now is going back to sleep."

"But I'm not tired."

"I was talking about myself," said Nat.

Leaving the room, Paul said, "Just for a change, like" in his most put-upon voice.

Go to hell, thought Nat, trying to part the waves of sleep's red sea.

Meanwhile, without any announcement that he was going out, Paul grabbed his coat from the bannister newel, and ventured out into the cruelly cutting Mondayness that surrounded their lovenest. He had almost forgotten why he, a creative person of the last bed, was up so early—without even the mid-term pregnancy of a Full English Breakfast. He thought of Nat, the business man, forever sucking his pencil over columns of sexless figures. Ever rising inordinately early (except today) for the chorus of dawn traders and hedge fund managers on talk radio. Something was happening to Nat, Paul was sure of it.

Paul was after someone. Someone who only flourished and luxuriated in the rarefied world of bleary-eyed Monday mornings. Someone who would be the protagonist of his drowning story. And someone who spent his or her whole life existing on the breadline of earliness, during hours so small they even defaulted and diminished to the white dot on an old-fashioned TV screen.

Eventually, after much tussling with the palate-corroded fixing of his face in the steamed up bathroom mirror, Nat climbed into his car, and hissed a prayer into the rear-view mirror. The car had been playing up for the last fortnight, and even now, as it started, it went into a series of gulps or curtsies. But finally the engine mumbled an acquiescence. Nat reversed out into the avenue. His head was full of two jealous sets of information, but the one he must concentrate on for now was that of the financial liberties being taken by certain members of staff.

He parked. The engine coughed at him as he got out of the car and dragged his chubby briefcase free. A sideways rain was falling; the wind was nipping chips out of his temples. The lobby was warm. He was greeted by ancillary staff, and returned each greeting warmly, fully conscious of the relevant name no more than a minute later. He climbed the stairs.

Surprisingly Katie Lenglert was waiting in his outer office. "Good morning, Nathaniel," she said, her accent like a tickle. Nat had always found her attractive. "Would you have a moment?"

"I was going to be calling for you this morning," Nat replied, non-committally. "Could I just have a moment to get a coffee."

"I'll get it," Katie replied. "Black, two sugars, yes?"

"Yes," Nat replied. She knows she's up the Swannee, he thought. Bit late now for all that, love, he went on. Your goose is cooked. Never mind a *disciplinary*; you're lucky if I don't call the police. He hung his coat, played his voicemail and checked his diary. The coffee came, in the hands of a contrite Katie Lenglert. As she sat, Nat realised that she'd even chosen a short skirt for the occasion. He wanted to put his hand up to see if she wore suspenders, because he couldn't quite see. The thought of Paul stopped him, as it always did, when he found himself sinking into that sexual lounge lizard mind-set where every-body of every gender under the sun was yearning for his fumbling attentions...

Beating about no bush whatsoever, Nat said, "It's about your expenses."

Katie paused. "What is? What about them?"

Nat frowned. "Isn't that why you wanted to see me?"

"No. Have I done something wrong?"

"Well, you haven't done much right, to tell you the truth," he replied. "But why did you want to see me?" If not to apologise and beg forgiveness.

"Well . . . " she said weirdly ". . . it's about your destiny."

"Excuse me?" Was Destiny an account that the firm was working on?

"You heard me. Are you sure you know what shape your destiny's taking?"

"I'm not sure I follow," Nat said.

"It's about the dream you had last night."

"The dream?"

"That's right. It's time, Nathaniel. And would you do me a favour and stop repeating?"

A considerable effort was required not to do so. The dream from last night was a nice warm wash, and it flowed through him now: he had heard the heavens, jamming on an odd karaoke. Suddenly Nathaniel had the impression that he hadn't woken up. In an attempt to restore some order he went on, "There are serious errors of judgement on your expenses forms."

To which Katie's reply was unequivocal. "Fuck my expenses form," she said. "You've got close, and you don't even know you've done it."

"Done what? Close to what?"

"To the secrets. Jesus, Nat. Wake up."

"Go slowly."

"We've been watching you for some time now."

Rooted in Nat's breast, there was still a sense of curdled pride. That was something like the sentence that he had intended to use. Once more he attempted to redress the balance of superiority. "I could say the same thing," he mumbled lamely.

"Yes, Nat, keep going." She sounded weary. "Even in the face of something bigger than your ego, you can't quite bring yourself to stop being a *putz*, can you?"

"Sticks and stones."

And Katie shook her head. "I'm beginning to find you pathetic, Nat. Just listen. You're close enough for us to be able to use you. Don't bother with any witty repartee, for Christ's sake. We've been waiting for a while."

Deciding to bite, for the sake of a peaceful morning if for no other reason, Nat said, "Okay. Who's 'we'?"

"Paul and I."

"Paul who?"

"Your partner—Paul. The man who shares your bed every night?"

Jealousy rang its silly bell. The French for Venetian Blind was Jalousie, he somehow recalled from school French. "And how the hell do you know Paul?" Nat asked, blinking.

"Aren't you warm in here?" Katie enquired.

"Getting warmer by the second. Answer my question, if you'd be so kind."

"Okay. Here comes the difficult part." Katie paused. "I met Paul under the sea—the North Sea. It was bloody freezing, I can tell you. And then again I met him in a stream; this was a few years later . . ."

Nat interrupted. "You know, I could call for security."

"We drowned, Nat. Paul and I drowned."

Nat's eyeballs swelled. He was cross, but he had got to the point where he had to know the answers. "Explain your understanding of drowned," he said.

"I mean, he and I took water into our lungs and we *died*. Is that clear enough?" Katie met Nat's gaze with full hostility. Then she softened. "Sorry. You might imagine, talking about the day you passed away on is hardly a happy topic."

"I can imagine."

"People talk a lot of nonsense, Nat, about those moments," said Katie. "It's *not* a tunnel of light—or at least it wasn't for us. It was very much like an acceptance. And do you know what I saw? I saw a constellation of stars, and I heard voices: they were trying to tell me something. But I couldn't get it. I couldn't get there."

"Where does Paul fit into this?" Nat asked.

"Well, at the time he didn't fit in anywhere: I was nine years old. Family holiday in Scotland. Unbelievably, I still think, I decided to go into the water. Anyway, the rest writes itself. I found the Chamber, although it was only years later that I heard it called that."

"And what is it?"

"It's the room you go to when you're drowning, to put it simply. You go there, and only part of you comes back. My parents dragged a nine year-old's body from the waves, but part of me took up residence in the Chamber. If residence is the right word. Imprisonment might be closer to the truth. You're in there until another poor bugger ends his life in the same place."

"And this was Paul, right."

"Right."

"Well, I don't want to burst your bubble," said Nat, "but Paul's never even been to Scotland. We have a conversation like this every time I say how much I liked going up there as a student. He says he'd rather have his nipples chewed off than go to the frozen north. I don't feel I'm misquoting him with that either."

Katie crossed her legs, as if she knew that Paul was diminishing to a blind point of light, and would not be able to protect her from Nat's advances . . . unless she bolstered up the image of Paul with further fictions. "The man you now know of as Paul might never have been to Scotland, but a part of him has, and that part died. His name was Jim, or James. He was an artist. He did the dumb artist thing. Woman doesn't want me—what the hell? I'll kill myself. And he did that."

"So what was your name, before you were Katie?"

"Jean," said Katie. "Are you trying to trick me?"

"I'm just waiting you out, Katie, and trying to see where this is all going."

"I already told you where it's going. It's going to your destiny."

"Forgive me, I forgot." There was no disguising the bitterness in Nat's tones. "So he came to rescue you, did he?"

"That's right. He drowned in exactly the same place, so he was able to do that. The part of me that'd seen the skies and the part of him that had seen the skies were freed from the Chamber, and we joined the composite bodies that you know and love: Katie and Paul."

"I don't love you," said Nat.

"And you don't know Paul," said Katie. "But that's by the bye. We're both of us made up of drowned souls, Nathaniel, and we're trying to get home—we're trying to find the way to the place you saw in your dreams."

"How many souls? How many souls are inside you?"

"Thousands. Another one joins—a man for Paul and a woman for me, it always seems to be—every time one or the other rescues the other one. Do you follow me?"

"In Scotland?"

"No. There are millions and millions of Chambers in this country alone. Where there's water, there might be a drowning; and where there's a drowning there's the possibility of a Chamber. And then the possibility of a subsequent rescue."

There was no conversation for a good few seconds. Nat despised being spoken to by his staff in any tones other than respectful ebullience, but he couldn't stop himself listening to this woman—nor looking at her—nor posing the dangerous question.

"So what do you imagine this all has to do with me?" he asked.

Katie's reply was immediate. "You've been going there regularly since you were a child," she said. "You've been going there, but you've forgotten it all. What we want to know is how the hell you've been doing it without a single drop of water entering your mouth."

Nat's number was up. He had snapped.

Snapped and became two. Or even three. Or more. The audit trail was vague but certainly discernible amid the trial and tribulations of his own blind past, now clarifying, crystallising . . . A lifetime flashes before your eyes, they say, upon the point of drowning . . . but they (whoever *they* were) had got it the wrong way round; only upon waking from that dead core of nothingness into existence did a full lifetime fleet by and become your own . . .

Nat touched the top of his head and felt a path to the brain . . . a brain called Paul or Jim, he wasn't sure; yet it was sticky to the touch and the touch itself sent his eyes revolving like a fruit machine's barrels, and his mind cascaded into a waterfall. The woman cost far too much. She knew no economies of truth.

The universe of straw, clutching, grasping the nettle that was Nat. He tipped his head back on his neck and poured the hot coffee into his mouth, with the cup an inch from his lips. He had to drown; he had to go now. The coffee gurgled in the throat-well, and Nat spluttered.

"Come with me," he said, standing up with coffee printed on his chin.

Katie stood. She smoothed her skirt. A worried expression was on her face.

There was something very restrictive about the uni in universe, and until now a secret had been kept about quite how private it was. Nat stepped forward and took Katie in his arms; her expression changed to a madwoman's rictus of rage. However, no words could Nathaniel hear; his ears were full of water, and blood, and singing.

Closing his eyes allowed him to escape to the letting Chamber, where he could unsquare the circle and do himself a favour: he could write words, a bathful of words, which would fizz like his early morning nosebleeds, when he'd try to swim under the waves for too long—until his head would ring with the pressure.

And the pleasure: the ecstasy of the lightshows behind his eyes.

Paul, Nathaniel knew, would have been so proud. But Paul had died a long time earlier.

HUSH HUSH LITTLE KITTY

by DARREN SPEEGLE

Calendar year CC060, A-Dam on Uram. Central Port bustling with the comings and goings of tourists. Inside, the subtle fragrance of the air conditioning system; outside, the smell of crumbling fungus acrid on the mizzly air . . . staler for the weight of the moisture, which seemed to hold it in place against a useless breeze.

Unhappy faces as arrivals were forced to cross the distance between Landing and Receiving in the open air, thank you most graciously to a malfunction in the long tunnel to and from which all gangways led. The paneled glass facade that was the end to this particular inconvenience appeared to ripple like broken water as it accepted these unhappy faces into the giant main structure of Central Port.

Inside the hall, at Receiving, a sweeping arcing graffito scrawled over the entryway announced: *HUSH, HUSH, LITTLE KITTY, AND YOU'LL HEAR IT WHISPERING BACK.* The words appeared to have been sprayed across the wall, shimmering delicately in the light of the overheads, exhibiting a strange iridescence, harbouring a strange meaning. Welcome to A-Dam on Uram. Check your psyches in at the main counter.

The river of bodies leading there, the various styles and cultures, the wide, eager eyes...and lost in it all, myself.

Myself . . . and the one who suddenly accosted me. An imparter of information, you know the type, inclined to brief me on the queer opalesque greeting that stared down at me.

"You know, man, if the power was shut down right now-you speak standard?—OK, if the whole port went black, you would find that message still glowing. You know why? Because it's biological, man. They keep the shit in tanks, and spray it like paint. Only it's not paint. It's *alive*. It's alive in the tanks, it's alive on the wall. See the fuzzy edges—"

Cut off as he was struck by a passing shoulder. Cursing as he turned back to me.

"Where was I?"

Where indeed. Stoned maybe, as I took him in. As I studied this moving photograph of him, gesture and garb. Certainly that look about him. That look of the free spirit, as my grandfather had referred to them. That same look, in fact, that the travel agent had worn.

I said, "The fuzzy edges."

"Yeah." A hesitant chuckle. "You get that too, do you? When you look at things?"

"Excuse me. I must be on my way."

"Yeah. Yeah, right. But hey, this your first visit to A-Dam?"

"Yes."

Regarding me wisely: "Do yourself a favour. Heed what it says. Take a moment and just listen. Listen beyond the surface clutter"—leaning in, as though to keep the secret between us—"and *you'll hear it whispering back*."

Then my imparter of information—yes, we all know the type—straightened up, satisfied with himself as he received a nod from me.

"I'll do that." And moved on my way.

Two hours later, and the bathroom mirror in Room 301, The Omni, etched with the little narcissisms we do ourselves before venturing out into new territory. The lobby door whispered to behind me, and the charm and city lay before.

A-Dam on Uram was a beehive of activity, its tourism market in flowering array. I had been told it was a close replica of its mother city, and so it seemed to me, although I had never been to Terra's Amsterdam—which of course is off-limits now. What need, with the library of discs the travel agent had made available to me, with the memories of my grandfather, once stationed there, once in love with the place and its museums. Aesthetically anyway, Uram's copycat Mecca of tourism was exactly as I had imagined it-from the canals, the street lamps and the naughty window offerings right down to the expressions on the faces of the free-spirited mix of folk who thronged the place. All as advertised, all as remembered.

At least so far as my imagination could fit the pieces together.

I could not have known, for instance, precisely how a café would smell, with the smoky odours of its menu's herbal selections permeating the den's secret, moody confines. I could not have named the people glorified in its glass-protected antique posters, nor the artists whose eerie music bled from the boxes posted in no particular order about the hazy place.

No, I could only let my senses enhance the picture I had painted, and that to only a degree—then participation was required.

At my request, the recommendation. The recommendation, the substance *lustre*—as I had thought it might be.

Half of this corner of the galaxy recommended it. As such products went, this one had two distinct pluses. One, no harmful side effects; and two, the coming forth of who you really were. It was the second I was more interested in, although honestly I thought the whole thing a scam. I was more than a little suspicious of substance enhancers, especially when it came to their effect upon my identity. For if I wasn't who I thought I was, then why be at all?

Who I thought I was, as it turned out, was still who I was—only without the static, the noise . . . the "clutter," as my hippie friend at Receiving had put it.

When I requested my check, I happened to drop my fist against the rubbery surface of the table, and a cloud of fine dust, very strong in smell, rose from the spot.

Stepping out of the café, I took in the fresh air, mizzly though it was. The acridness I had noticed before seemed so slight now, after the smoky interiors of the café, that it was hardly detectable. And yet it *was* detectable, to my heightened senses, and catching it in my nostrils made me remember the words that had welcomed me to this place. Amusing myself as much as anything else, I did as the graffito had instructed. I paused to listen. But just as the surface distractions were beginning to fade into the background, a woman stepped up to me.

She was lovely and soft, luminous hair, crystal eyes, and all the melodious substance of my mood.

"Who are you?" she asked.

I smiled at her. "That is a good question."

"Here . . . " she said, and placed in my hand a spongy object, a growth.

"What is this?" I asked.

"What isn't it?" she said rhetorically. She looked into my eyes as she spoke—which wouldn't have been a thing, of itself, except that we were both participants.

"So . . . "

"So?" she echoed.

"So why are your eyes so bright on such a dreary day?"

"Hush," she said.

I did.

She watched me as I listened, and it seemed to me that she was listening, too, without trying, watching me.

As the noises of commercial A-Dam began to slip away, so did her command of me, that subtle, powerful effect of her as I stood before this woman, a victim of my senses.

"What is your name?" I reached, fearing I would lose her to the rising storm.

"Shhh. Listen."

I did, and I heard.

She touched my ear.

I heard it whispering back.

"Where is it coming from?" I asked her.

"There." She pointed at a sign. Its announcement spray-painted, so it appeared, and yet shivering in the awareness of itself.

"And there." Another.

"There!" She pointed at the thing in my hand. I looked at it, was certain it had begun to move. I resisted the urge to toss it away, to let the image of it writhing in my palm overtake me.

"Thank you," I said, handing it back to her, "but I have one of my own."

She smiled. "My name is Sha."

We walked along the crowded street, together, neither of us having invited the other, and the whole affair that was A-Dam on Uram stretching out before us like so much romance for the taking. We dodged bicycles, tossed coins to the colourful blankets of sidewalk musicians, amusedly declined the invitations of sprucely-dressed vendors and their often human wares. Together we visited another café, contributing to our certain *lustre* while enjoying the company of each other, without much talk, without much pressure, without the constraints of time or any of those other considerations that might stand out there in the way of pleasure and relaxation. We dined at a place called *Spores*, starting on sauteed mushrooms and moving on to a delicious something covered in mushroom sauce. We drank a bitter-tasting tea and desserted on a puffy "organic" bitter-tasting cake, and all the while loving it and complimenting the chef and laughing for the sheer joy of living the lustrous life.

When we were out among the busy sidewalks again, and evening settling over the city, she pulled me to her with almost an urgency.

Whispering, "Where has the day gone?"

I couldn't tell her.

"Will we roam all night?"

"Wherever you wish."

And somehow we were away from there, and in her place, the sheets and the overhead fluorescence. Her elegance and my newly discovered freedom...

She sat atop me, naked. And mathematics were too severe, physics too limiting.

"So . . ."

"So."

"When my holiday is done . . . "

"We must return to our lives."

"It doesn't have to be so final."

After that first dialogue we had shared, strangers outside a café, I was never completely sure which one of us spoke, which one of us brought the thought to the surface.

"No, I suppose it doesn't."

"Then . . . "

She lowered herself to me, letting her breasts, the necklace she wore fall against my chest. We embraced tightly-lovingly, I thought, as I knew I was taking her back with me.

And then she was sitting again, the pressure of her thighs against my legs, the terrible beauty of her nearly overwhelming me.

I touched her necklace, pieces of grey pulpy matter strung along a chain.

"We only bloom for a day, you know."

"I know."

And that was enough. If it was all, it was enough.

There were no special arrangements to be made. Visas were a dime a dozen in this place. She might as well have been from here as anyplace else, and I suspected she had been here a long time. I noticed as we boarded the ship that she carried with her the scent of the place. She was smoking before we had set off. The stewardess said it was a nonrestrictive flight, she even brought us a pipe, and a package of the scented combustible crystals that aided in the burning of the stuff. I shared part of Sha's necklace with her as we were lifting off. We brought no more. On the other side of the galaxy it was forbidden.

We arrived on Abar Seven as the sun was completing its cycle. A pinkish glow possessed the northern skies, and the land was cast in a weird silvery-pink light. As we walked from the port toward the parking pad, I threw my arms wide, which was my way of welcoming my Sha to her new home. But she looked away to the north and the fading skies and said quietly, "Hush, hush, little kitty . . . "

"We are not on Uram any longer," I reminded her.

"Shhh . . . listen."

I did as she bid, humouring her, thinking it would take some time to acclimatise her. At first I heard nothing, nothing unusual . . . then . . .

The whispering seemed to come from all around us, as though it had always been here, as though our arrival had nothing to do with it. I turned to Sha, who had fallen behind, and found her on the ground, on her knees, her arms failing her as she tried to reach out to me. Before my eyes she began to wilt, as from the strenuous task of living. The material of her, the flesh of her, becoming spongy, dry, brittle beneath the retreating eye of the day.

LARVAL TUESDAY

by DAVID ALEXANDER

I did my first yuppie scum with a sharpened pencil. It was around seven o'clock in the morning. It was in TriBeCa, where there are now a lot of yuppie scums. It was on the corner of some street and Greenwich Avenue. I was sleeping near there, inside a condemned building full of dead cats. I usually sleep at Planet Homeless, which is what we all call the shantytown under the Manhattan Bridge near the old South Street piers but sometimes I get drunk and wander around. I got the pencil the night before. It was already sharpened when I got it.

A number two pencil made by cheap foreign labour. She was this well-dressed bitch walking near the men's shelter on 44th off Lex. I asked her if she could spare some change and she gives me the pencil. It was already sharpened. Smiled at me like fuck you piece of shit and keeps walking, turns into Grand Central. But I keep the pencil, I didn't throw it away. Pencil was telling me something but I couldn't figure out what until just before I used it.

Got enough change to buy myself a bottle of Wild Irish Rose and kept walking. I liked the pencil. I kept feeling the pencil in my pocket then I would take it out and look at it now and then. It was different. The different was on one end sharp pointy tip hard black, on the other end round pink soft you can press with thumb, in middle yellow ridged hard smooth shiny you can turn inside now.

I keep taking pencil out looking at pencil. Then sometime it late, remember what Lembu tell me about Kansas City pencil trick and how he show me how to hold the pencil in my hand so I could do a motherfucker with the pencil so fast the motherfucker wouldn't even know what hit him.

Around seven o'clock next morning, I get up and count my change. I need another dollar fifty for my next bottle. It still early but the yuppie scums are on their way to work. I'm watching the yuppie scums floating real light just above the sidewalk so it looks like they walking but they ain't.

They float, yuppie scums. They devils floating on the sidewalks of Manhattan. You know the devil floats because he come from hell and he full of fire so he don't weigh too much. These yuppie scums devils you can tell a lot of them wear sneakers to fool you so you think they walk when they really float.

I see one yuppie scum with nice fresh face. He wearing eyeglasses and got nice new suit on. Briefcase swings when he walks this yuppie scum. I go up to him and I say, "Spare some change, man?" But this yuppie scum keep walking. I go after this devil yuppie and I say, "Hey, man. You hear what I say? I ask if you can spare some change?" Devil scum keep floating in his Gucci loafers.

I look around. Nobody looking. I have Kansas City trick pencil in my hand in my coat pocket. I grab yuppie scum's arm do it just like Lembu show me.

Sag sag yuppie, I think. Sag now yuppie scum. You dead. I look around but still nobody's watching. Yuppie dead right outside dead cat building on Greenwich Avenue where I sleep sometime and I drag him inside where nobody lives but the dead cats. Everybody knows about the dead cats in TriBeCa. The cops too, they know about the dead cats. I know cops know because I work for the cops at the precinct as a janitor's assistant.

You ask them about this building, they know it, because them dead cats stink up the whole fucking block. Old lady used to live in the building and when she die, they find she keep hundreds of cats. These cats diseased and give each other diseases.

When these diseased cats die, old lady throw them down in the basement. They find hundreds of cat corpses in basement. They clean it out but dead cat stink never go away.

I strip off clothes from dead devil yuppie with my pencil inside and I look at his face. I think to myself that this yuppie's face look like my own face. I strip off clothes from me and put on dead pencil thing. I drag yuppie down to basement where cats stink and throw him down cat pit so he stink with the cats. Nobody look for this devil in his own stink pit for a long time.

Now I take dead clothes and put clothes on me I look inside yuppie's wallet and see what he has. Two hundred in cash, Visa Gold and American Express. Diners Club. Drivers license. In briefcase I find business papers show me this yuppie is stockbroker on his way to company in Wall Street when I put my pencil in his Kansas.

I put on devil yuppie's clothes and take his briefcase in my hand. He has my pencil inside him. I walked down to Seventh Avenue South where I hailed a cab. The number was on South Street, big building. I heard my pencil inside him where the devil stunk with the cats. I knew that pencil and what it said. I nodded at the security motherfucker at the desk. I took the elevator up with the other yuppie scums. I went into the devil's office and sat at his desk.

I could not float like the devil but they did not notice. When I said motherfucker motherfucker you devil motherfucker they heard his yuppie voice from my lips because of my pencil inside.

All day I do the yuppie's work. I talk like the yuppie, make trades and take the yuppie's commissions. Nobody knows who I am because I look like the yuppie.

He said my name was Stewie. He wore a white shirt like mine and a wide crazy tie. She said my name was Stewie. Her name was Leslie. His name was George. She wore a striped business suit like a man's but a dress. He said my name was Stewie. His name was William I called him Bill. He who said my name was Stewie first whose name was George said we should have a drink after work he wanted to talk to me before I started my vacation.

"So you're getting away to Antigua again, you lucky sonofabitch," George said to me as we sat at the bar of a bar at the South Street Seaport named Mellville. "Wish I could get away."

"Why the hell don't you, guy?" I tell George. "You've got vacation time coming."

"It's not that. It's Jessica. She teaches English and she only gets off summers. So it has to be June and July for us. Ah, to be single again."

"It's no bed of roses," I said to him.

"Yeah, true. But the ability to pick yourself up in the middle of December and get the hell out of New York to an island in the Caribbean makes up for a multitude of shortfalls, my friend."

George ordered another scotch and soda.

"Yeah, I guess you've got a point."

"So where exactly are you staying in Antigua?" George asked.

"I booked the Hilton at Dead Man's Cove," I told George. "I was there before last year. I liked it a lot. It's right near some good wrecks I want to dive on."

"Yeah, that's right, you're into that. Shit, it must be scary. I remember a couple of years ago Jessica and I went to Cancun for ten days and we went snorkling and I saw this enormous barracuda just hanging there in the water looking at us. And I remember how scared shit I suddenly was because you weren't supposed to go swimming wearing a watch because the shine of the dial could attract barracuda."

"Uh huh," I said.

"So I had just bought this new Rolex Oyster, which cost me almost two thousand bucks, okay? And there was just no damned way I was going to leave the watch in our room where the wetback maid could steal it so I kept it on when we snorkelled."

"You could've put it in the hotel safe."

"I don't trust those either, not Mexican ones, anyway," George said, sipping his drink and eating some nuts from the dish. "So I had the watch on and I knew there were supposed to be barracuda in the lagoon but when we dived twice before we didn't see any so I figured it was just bullshit.

"Then that last time I see this big, mean fish with these sharp teeth looking at me. I guess it was attracted by the watch because it came at me like a torpedo and I remember thinking to myself let it eat Jessica don't let it eat me let it eat Jessica not me but fortunately it didn't get either of us I guess it wasn't hungry but if it had better Jessica than me."

"Yeah, you should never wear anything that glitters underwater," I told George who had said nothing about his shit cowardly prayer but my pencil put in the devil told me. "I wear this special diving watch with a Velcro patch over the face when I scuba."

"I still don't see how you can do it. The mere thought about how I had to fight off that barracuda with my flipper while I pushed Jessica ahead of me makes me cringe at the mere thought of ever going swimming again."

"George," I told him. "It's just like the business. No risk, no reward."

"Yeah, I guess," he said, too drunk by now to remember what we were talking about anyway.

We shot the breeze awhile and then George and me headed to the IRT stop on Broadway and Adams, which we both took uptown. I got off in two stops. George, who lived on the West Side, kept going, promising to keep tabs on my accounts and call my answering service if any problems he couldn't handle came up while I was away. I check the digital yuppie devil watch I wear. It says I have plenty of time to get over to the cop station to do the night shift.

I don't have to anymore because I am now yuppie devil but there are some things I want to get only cop station has. I go upstairs to dead yuppie's loft apartment in TriBeCa and take off shit suit shit tie shit shoes look for something real to wear when I go out again. Find jeans, sneakers, parka, sweatshirt. These will do me.

Then I go in shower and get clean like I do at men's shelter before I show up at cop station to work. I come out of the shower naked and see faggot motherfucker watching me. I know this faggot mother-fucker from my pencil in devil put. He live here with me I know. He back from faggot yuppie job in public relations.

"You should have waited till I got home," he said. "We could have both taken a shower."

"We can take another one."

"Mmm, great idea," faggot motherfucker says and comes over to me naked reaches for my dick I shove Kansas City faggot kicks like barracuda then goes limp. I take dead faggot roommate and bend his body double so his spine cracks. I fold his legs up over his face and stick this dead yuppie roommate inside a big black garbage bag I take from the basement of the building.

I get dressed in comfortable clothes. I put the bag inside a refrigerator carton I find in basement with the trash. I put the refrigerator carton on a shiny red hand truck. I wheel the hand truck in the dark down to the dead cat building on Greenwich Avenue corner of and dump dead faggot yuppie in the devil's hole with my pencil like the first.

I get on bus on Sixth Avenue. Bus takes me down to cop station where I work as janitor's assistant. I work the night shift, eight till three. I don't sleep, I don't care. I just work the night shift. Nobody bother me on the night shift. I do what I want. I know one cop motherfucker who I had watched several times during the course of the two months I worked at the precinct.

He had not been sufficiently security-conscious to guard the combination of his padlock from my watchful eyes. Cop motherfucker thought I was a retard. I let all the cop motherfuckers think so. I knew the combination to the officer's locker which held within it all his gear. Cap, jacket, patrol belt, holster, nightstick, shield and other paraphernalia. When I leave cop station that morning, I carrying all the motherfucker's gear in a bag.

It still dark now. Before it get light, I downtown under the Manhattan Bridge on the South Street piers where I have my shack in Planet Homeless. I go inside and my bitch is waiting. I fuck my bitch because she wants me to fuck her. I fuck her hard so she moans and make everybody know she my bitch and I tell her all this shit about how I got a raise and maybe we can get in that program where we can get an apartment now. She happy to hear that shit and I go to sleep holding my bitch on her tits the way she likes me to.

I wake up. It late in the morning and my bitch she gone already looking for bottles with her big black garbage bag over her shoulder. She leave me can of beer to drink. She leave me cigarettes. I drink the beer and smoke my cigarette. Then I go look for Lembu. I find Lembu under the bridge and I tell Lembu, yo man I can get you a lot of good swag you can fence.

Lembu says, yeah, really? No shit, man, I say. Jewellery, credit card numbers, electronic shit, laptops, antique vases, plumbing fixtures, maybe even cars. Can you use the shit? Damn sure can, he tells me. Lembu wears a beeper. When I'm ready with some shit for him, I should call him up.

I go back to dead yuppie loft apartment to shower and change. I have an appointment this morning. The building was a high-rise near the Flatiron building. She freeze-dried rich bitch. I have an appointment to see some prime Manhattan real estate this morning. She meet me in the lobby and shake my hand. I'd phoned the previous day in response to an ad in the Sunday Times real estate section for Chelsea apartments. I looking for yuppie scum to do.

"You look wet," she told me as I shook off my Burberry raincoat and draped it over a chair in her office, where we had gone for her to get a prospectus and layout plan for me. "Is it raining that hard?"

"Hard as Chinese algebra. And if you think I look wet, you should see my canoe and the four native rowers who got me here," I told her motherfucker bitch bitch motherfucker bitch but she heard yuppie shit from the pencils in devils that came out of my mouth like fire honey words.

She laughed as she picked up her keys and we went up in the elevator to the penthouse apartment. A yuppie scum devil with fresh milk face let us in. He was talking to another yuppie scum on a cellular flip phone in yuppie shit voice.

I shook the hand of the yuppie scum and the freeze-dried real estate lady take us around, making a big deal out of the shit view of Gramercy Park on one side and the Flatiron building on the other. Motherfuckers when you sleep in the park and on Fourteenth Street by the bank like me motherfuckers you don't think that view worth shit I say but because I yuppie devil now it come out, "These views are really spectacular."

"And the view of the park also gives you an added dimension of psychological space," the real estate bitch told me.

"Yes, that's certainly true," I said. "I hadn't been able to put it into so many words, but that's exactly what I'd been thinking as I looked out the window."

I was shown the bathroom with its built-in whirlpool nozzles in the tub, the three closets, one of which had built-in storage drawers for sweaters, pants, socks and scarves, the kitchenette with its built-in Whirlpool dishwasher and cabinetry of fine Norwegian wood, the working fireplace and the amusing display niches suitable for the display of valuable antiques and objets d'art. We discussed the asking price, applicable real estate taxes and monthly carrying charges. I shook hands with the yuppie devil and the freeze-dried bitch and went back out into the pouring rain.

It still rain when I come back that night in my stolen cop uniform, flashing stolen cop badge. I bang on yuppie devil door and tell him to let me in right away. Yuppie opens door as wide as chain lets him and asks me what's wrong. His woman stand behind him. They both in robes. I show him my stolen cop badge and tell him there may be a pervert hiding in his penthouse apartment let me in. As soon as yuppie devil opens door, I club him with my billy.

I move so fast I club the woman too before she can even move. I take one of my bitch's big black garbage bags out of my pocket and shake it open. Starting with the rings on yuppies' fingers, I go around the apartment stuffing whatever shit I can stuff into the garbage bag.

I go back outside and press button on car alarm remote, watching taillights of a black BMW down the street flash. I put my garbage bag inside BMW trunk and hide car keys and alarm remote under the left rear bumper. Then I call Lembu's beeper on my cell phone. He call me right back and I tell him there a car with a trash bag full of swag inside and where to get the alarm remote.

Every day job think yuppie devil on my vacation to Antigua I finding more yuppies to do and rob through Manhattan real estate agents. I go wherever yuppies live. Upper East Side, Lower East Side. Soho, Noho, Broho, TriBeCa. West Side. Real estate agents take me everywhere, show me everything. Every night I come back in stolen cop uniform, flash stolen cop badge, swing stolen cop Kevlar baton, do yuppie devils wherever they run or hide.

I steal rings, microwaves, cellular phones, televisions, answering machines, cash, gold, books, magazines, whatever I can stuff into one of my bitch's big black garbage bags. I go outside and use alarm remotes to look for tail light flash to find yuppies' cars. I call Lembu's beeper service on cellular flip phone to tell Lembu where to find cars with garbage bags full of stolen yuppie swag in car trunks. Then I go back to Planet Homeless where my bitch is waiting for me, and I fuck my bitch like she wants it and then I go to sleep.

The next morning I take the money from Lembu he get from all the stolen merchandise. I give away some of the money to the people under the bridge, but the rest of it I keep for myself and I hide it away in a special place where only I can find it.

Then I go back to pencil devil's apartment where I shower and change my real clothes into yuppie shit clothes and make an appointment with another real estate agent so I can find more yuppies to do and rob and take more of their shit for Lembu to sell.

One night I just do a bunch of yuppie scums at a townhouse in Yorkville. I come out the door into the street wearing my stolen cop uniform with my black garbage bag over my shoulder and the alarm remote in my hand. I squeeze the button and look for the red blink lights up the block when somebody says my name. I turn around and see who recognise me despite late night and stolen cop uniform.

"Stewie, is that you?"

"Hello, George," I say to yuppie scum coworker from my Wall Street job office. "Pretty late to be walking around, isn't it?"

"Yeah."

"So how come you're out?"

"Let's just call it a little family dispute and leave it at that," George answered me. "But what the hell are you doing dressed like a cop? And how come you're not in Antigua? Who's that Lexus belong to anyway?"

I lean close upside George's face like I gonna whisper something in his ear.

"I'm the barracuda of death, George, and I'm looking for somebody to bite on the ass," I tell him and give him the Kansas City pencil fast so he shivers then his knees buckle under him. I drag George over to the Lexus belong to the yuppie scums in the townhouse and throw George in the trunk. Then I throw the black garbage bag full of yuppie devil swag on top of him and hear my cell phone ring.

"Where the shit be at?" ask Lembu.

"First Avenue. Corner by the light. Silver Lexus. Remote in the usual spot."

"Got you, man."

"Stiff in the trunk," I add.

"No prob," Lembu say. "I take care of the motherfucker."

I put away the flip phone in my pocket. I had enough of this yuppie shit for a lifetime. I made my money, I got in my licks. Now I go back to my bitch and fuck her hard the way she likes it and tomorrow after I drink my beer and smoke my cigarette maybe we go get on the program.

THE ENTHRONED REMEMBER

by FORREST AGUIRRE

"It's him!" Van Klanker yelled as he wrestled the black giant out of the underbrush. Their weapons, a blood-coated assegai and hot barrelled rifle, fell atop each other as the men grappled. More pith helmets bobbed above the fray: three, four, five—arms pummelling pistons, boots cracking bones. The giant gave way under the incessant thumping.

"Jina laku ni nani?" Van Klanker screamed into the ebony face.

"Mitwundu."

"Says his name's Mitwundu."

"It's him alright!" A young, excited voice.

"Look at the scars—matches Frau Keller's description perfectly," an older settler, more measured.

Van Klanker looked more closely as the other Boers roped the behemoth's arms. Four sets of bumps on the forehead.

"Like horns," the youngster again. "Seems we caught the devil himself."

"Frau Keller's devil, anyway," Van Klanker dusted himself off, breathed the wet jungle air into his burning lungs, then picked up the weapons. "She'll have her justice soon, may Henrik rest in peace."

The others crossed themselves. "May Henrik rest in peace," they mumbled in unison.

The morning sun arced upward as they followed the Yamazi River south, toward the outpost town Ngome.

*

Diedre Keller stood in the plantation house doorway looking past her husband's fresh grave. A parade of laughing squatter children emerged from beneath the palm leaves on the main path leading to the sprawling abode, their afternoon dust cloud enshrouding the group that followed—a khaki-clad circle of settler militiamen surrounding an immense black warrior.

Frau Keller stared at the giant. She remembered that face, that body, those bound hands—how they had worked the soil, pulled the glistening body up the trees, split the bark that bled precious rubber into waiting buckets below. She had seen that body kneel before her husband's kiboko, the rhinoceros-hide whip scoring purple welts across the broad shoulders, the bulging back. And the face—grinning, straining as the arms and body crushed the life from her husband's throat, only relaxing after the decisive snapping of her beloved's neck, the servant becoming the master. That face, ignored until that point, had burned itself into her memory—four initiation scars across the wide dark forehead, eyes like coal pits, a broad, flat nose above the sharp ivory teeth. A demon. No less.

*

A rope was swung over a high branch, the noose secured and, within minutes, the paroxysms that shook Mitwundu's goliath frame slackened as the brain starved for lack of oxygen. Van Klanker stabbed through his huge heart with the warrior's own assegai as a gesture of finality. The tree rubbed raw under the weight of the body, the carcass swaying lightly in the breeze. Frau Keller stood near the dead man, looking up at his open, bulging eyes, his lolling tongue, staring even as the sun went down. The lynch mob dispersed, leaving her to process the satisfaction of vengeance, to enjoy the taste of justice.

As the last man left, she wept for the loss of her husband, balling her fists and spitting the words through clenched teeth: "Foul murderer! You have taken all that was mine—the truest husband that lived, a comfort to his wife, a man of honour and respect. My love! You robbed me of my love and my only joy is in your death—though your death is not worthy the life of my departed husband."

And she looked down and saw how her tears dripped upon the feet of the dead: The feet that had carried wood to her fire and food to her table, that had pattered back and forth playing games with the children—and she felt sorry for his death and felt compassion. And she looked up into the black pupils and noted a residue of soul, a life force in the un-functioning orbs and marvelled at the power that exuded from the servant Mitwundu when he lived, how he brought people alive wherever he walked, how his smile spread like contagion through a crowd.

*

The rope lashed out like a cobra as she severed the strands. The carrion fell to the ground with a thump, leaning with its torso against the tree as if the giant had lain there for a nap—with a noose entwined about his neck. Diedre looked again into his eyes and wept with such effort that she fainted, her cheek resting on his still chest. She awoke hours later as the dawn showed pink through the trees and she knew, when the desire for food and sleep had fled, when all her craving was to stare into his eyes and behold his peaceful face, that she loved him.

Only for a time did she leave him, returning with baskets full of clothes, flowers, jewellery and the great carved oak armchair that was her deceased husband's heirloom. Carefully, she dressed Mitwundu in her husband's best riding clothes: white shirt, khaki pants, knee-high bandages and boots all ill-fitting, undersize.

She wrestled the corpse into the armchair, placing a pipe in its hand and bucket-style frontier hat over its bald coal head. A ring of flowers, purple, yellow, white, rung the brim, a morbid celebration of life on death. She slipped her husband's wedding ring on the end of one enormous pinkie, then pierced the hanging tongue with diamond and pearl earrings—only unflawed words of beauty would fall from her new-found lover's mouth.

*

Visitors came often enough, mostly men who had come to seek her hand in marriage, as women—proper women—were few in the area surrounding Ngome. All of them left disappointed, spurned by the beauty—for she was not unattractive: red hair embraced her slender face, her blue eyes—spurned for their unworthiness, their inadequacies, when compared with her Mitwundu. When they saw how she doted on the decomposing corpse they fled in horror from her seeming insanity.

Rumours met with confirmations of rumour. Many wondered whether a demon had possessed the giant black body and bewitched the young maid. Her servants had abandoned her for the newly built factories of the southern cities. She was known by them as a sorceress, one who consorted with the dead, a necrophile. In town, gossipers shook their heads for the shame of it all.

Her actions could not be ignored for long. In time, a small group of settlers and missionaries, led by Van Klanker, went to Keller's plantation intent on burning the body and locking the crazed woman away in an asylum until she was cured of her delirium. They approached with stealth, stopping when they heard her voice up the path, speaking sweetly, almost in song, as a mother talks to her nursing baby:

*

"My love, strong and perfect warrior, knight, yes, knight, for I am your lady—consider my unworthy attentions and have pity on me. In life I truly knew you not, though I saw your face alive. Now, in death, I know you and beg of you to show compassion on me, a widow, who must live without a husband, while the ladies of your youth have surely forgotten you and now lie embraced in the arms of their lovers. But I, I remember you, and will not forget. Please, my love, remember me."

And she embraced him and sat on his rotting lap, her belly against his distended abdomen, and placed kisses on his cob-webbed mouth and ran her hands over the cracked and dry skin on the nape of his neck.

*

Van Klanker raised his rifle, the discharge crack echoing through the vaulted jungle, fading into eternity. The plans had changed—Frau Keller was beyond help, he thought. Diedre's head slumped to the corpse's shoulder, a neat hole through either side of her head. Her husband's shirt flooded red.

The mob set the house on fire after ransacking its contents, then threw their torches in a pile at the feet of the dead couple before treading back to town. The soot of the estate flames mixed with those of the Keller family heirloom, obscuring the harvest moon that rose over the uneven horizon. The fire, it was said, could be seen from the sea.

*

The embers cooled into glowing coals, blackened ruins mirroring the starry sky above. A leopard's roar in the night awoke Diedre. Her singed eyelids fluttered open and she looked upon her lover's disintegrated face through heat-bubbled eyes. She stroked her charred and flaking fingers across Mitwundu's open chest and he stirred.

"I have remembered you," the words rolled from his exquisitely jewelled tongue through his lipless burnt mouth. "I have remembered you, and I will not forget."

She smiled as the warm wind whistled through her skull-cavity and they walked together, hand-in-hand, into the forest of the night.

GLACIER

by D. HARLAN WILSON

One morning Rakehell Bartleberry walked outside of his house to retrieve the paper that was sitting on the bottom of his driveway. As he shuffled down the driveway in his slippers and robe, he noticed that the sun was abnormally bright. He didn't take the time to pause and scrutinize the sun, though, and it wasn't until he actually bent over to pick up the paper that he realized it wasn't the sun's fault everything was so bright, it was the fault of the glacier lying in his front yard. The glacier was very big and very white and was reflecting the sun's rays all over the place. The glacier itself, which might have been as large as the Hawaiian island Molokai, was all over the place, too.

Rakehell walked over to the foot of the glacier and frowned at it. "Where'd you come from?" he asked. The glacier didn't reply. Annoyed, he kicked it a little with his toes. "Get outta here," he told it. "Go on now. Scram."

*

The glacier didn't move a muscle. Its broad frontal lip lay there on top of his grass and the rest of its body lay there on top of the vast suburb that surrounded his grass. It wasn't melting either. A cloudless 75 degrees out today and the glacier, as far as Rakehell could tell, hadn't even broken a sweat. It worried him. If the glacier didn't melt, there was a good chance it would continue to make its way across his front yard and erode and ruin the whole damn thing. Rakehell spent a lot of time doing yardwork. He couldn't allow any of his neighbours to have a better-looking yard than his, and he liked how mowing the grass and trimming the hedges and pulling the weeds built up his muscles. He was also an incorrigible neat freak and had a tendency to pass out when things fell out of place. Whether these things happened to be runaway hairs on his meticulously combed head or runaway glaciers on his suburb and front lawn made no difference.

Rakehell kicked the glacier one more time before passing out. When he woke up, his face was sunburnt and the lip of the glacier was laying on top of his foot. "It's moving!" he yelled. A few seconds later he had a panic attack. The glacier had a firm grip on his foot and he didn't think he had the strength to pull it loose. But the panic attack lent him the necessary strength, and after he retrieved the foot he got up and ran inside his house.

"Mrs Bartleberry!" he screamed. "Mrs Bartleberry! Grab the prepubescents and pack our bags: we're leaving this place!" Mrs Bartleberry was Rakehell's wife. Her first name was Gwendolynne but he preferred to call her by her marital title. She would have liked him to call her Gwen, or better yet honey or darling, but she would rather have him call her Mrs Bartleberry and be happy than call her something else and be sad.

Mrs Bartleberry peeked her head out of the kitchen. "What's that dear?"

Rakehell stomped his foot on the wooden tiles of his foyer. One of the tiles broke. "I said let's go! LET'S GOOOO . . ." He passed out again. When he woke up, Mrs Bartleberry and their six prepubescents, Furter, Ianesco, Sublimina, Bartleberry, Gregious and Yicfung, were all looking down on him with puzzled expressions. Sublimina's puzzled expression had a hint of disgust in it. But not as much disgust as Rakehell had in his expression.

"Jesus H Christ," he griped, "can't I stay conscious for two seconds?"

The prepubescents looked at each other. Mrs Rakehell said, "What happened?"

*

Rakehell clumsily got to his feet. He stumbled around the living room for a few seconds in a daze, his family watching him with voyeuristic intensity. Then Rakehell steadied himself. He turned to his family and said, "There's a glacier in the front yard. I don't know where it came from and I don't know why it's here, but it's laying out there like a dead cow in the road and it won't go away. Not only that—it's moving. Not very fast, but it's moving all right, and it's headed right in our direction. So we have to leave. Do you understand?"

The puzzled expression returned to Mrs Bartleberry's face. The prepubescents, in contrast, all sprouted masks of fear.

"Are we going to die?" bleated Ianesco.

"I don't know," said Rakehell. "Maybe."

"You're scaring the prepubescents, dear," said Mrs Rakehell.

"Sorry."

Mrs Bartleberry cocked her head. "Are you?"

"Honestly? No. But at least I'm not lying to you people. Now listen, I want everybody and everything packed up in the SUV lickety-split. We may or may not have much time. That glacier's a slow mover but for all we know it could speed up and be going 80 miles per hour in the next few seconds, and I don't wanna be underneath that bastard when it's hauling ass like that. So let's get a move on!"

*

At that the Bartleberrys scattered like a cluster of ants that somebody's spit on. Twenty minutes later they were all inside the SUV. Rakehell and Mrs Bartleberry sat in the front seats with plenty of room to stretch out. The kids sat behind them, balled up in between the nooks and crannies of the furniture, appliances, clothing, toys, sporting equipment, booze and canned goods that had been crammed back there. Being balled up like that was very painful. All six of the prepubescents were crying, but they made sure to cry softly so that their father didn't get upset and pass out. The prepubescents were abnormally aware of and attentive to their parent's emotions, especially their father's, who, since he lacked the psychological capacity to internalize anything, externalized everything.

Rakehell placed the SUV in reverse and backed out of his garage and driveway. He hit the brakes. He placed the SUV in drive and drove forward . . . and ran into the glacier. "Shit," he said. He placed the car in reverse and backed into his driveway, hit the brakes, placed the car in drive and drove forward, this time in the other direction. But the other direction consisted of nothing more than a cul-de-sac encircled by square yellow houses with square green yards in front of them, and after Rakehell rounded it he ran into the glacier again. "We're trapped!" he exclaimed, and passed out. The prepubescents took the opportunity to cry louder than they've ever cried before, even louder than when they emerged from Mrs Bartleberry's womb. Mrs Bartleberry said, "There there, little ones," then popped a hot tamale in her mouth and blew on Rakehell's face until he woke up and the prepubescents toned down.

"Where am I, Mrs Bartleberry?" asked Rakehell.

"You're right here," she replied.

"Oh."

"Oh?"

"Yes. Oh."

"Daddy," said a purple-faced Yicfung. He was on the brink of suffocation and unable to stand it any longer. "I think I'm g-g-gonna die."

Rakehell turned around and looked behind him. "Behave yourself," he said. Then he backed the car up a little, told his wife and prepubescents to stay put, and got out.

*

The sky had yet to be tarnished by a cloud and the sun was much hotter now, but the glacier still wasn't melting. Rakehell strode over to it. He kneeled down in front of it, blinked at it . . . Nope, no wetness on the thing, no wetness at all; it was as milky and frosty and lackluster as any old Antarctic glacier.

"You should be gleaming with moisture," whispered Rakehell, shaking his head. "*Gleaming*, I'm telling you."

Disturbed, but not so disturbed that he was going to pass out again, not yet at least, Rakehell got to his feet. Except for the cul-de-sac, and the houses and yards surrounding the cul-de-sac, and his own house and yard (well, most of his yard), the glacier lay on top of everything, in every direction. It was as if, the night before, somebody had dropped a small, bright white mountain range on his suburb. But that was impossible, of course; the thing had to have crawled over here. But from where? The nearest glacier was something like 1000 miles away. Was he supposed to believe that it had crawled 1000 miles in one night, in . . . eight (give or take) hours? That means it must have been going 125 (give or take) miles per hour! No way, Rakehell told himself, although he couldn't help smirking at the prospect of a gigantic hunk of ice going that fast. The only other explanation he could think of was that the glacier had been hiding underground, underneath his suburb, and, for some reason, decided to come up last night. But how would it have come up? Unless there was a manhole the size of mountain range somewhere nearby, forget about it.

"I *despise* you," Rakehell told the glacier. As he turned to the SUV he thought he heard the glacier reply this time, but he was too full of hate to turn back around and confront it again.

*

"I think Yicfung's dead," said Mrs Bartleberry as Rakehell hopped back into the driver's seat and passed out. His wife didn't blow on him this time, but he woke up almost immediately, grumbling, "I thought I told you to mind your manners back there." He drove the SUV into the garage, closed the garage, considered cracking open all the windows and locking all the doors and keeping the SUV running for an hour or so, rejected the consideration, then ordered everybody to unload and unpack everything while he calmly retired to the wine cellar to get drunk. He unpacked his vast store of wine from the SUV himself . . .

In virtual darkness, Rakehell Bartleberry sat on a downy patch of cobwebs and guzzled bottle after bottle of his favorite wine, Inglenook sauvignon blanc, until he passed out. He stayed passed out for a while and had a nightmare about the glacier. It was extremely hypertense and gory, this nightmare, but his head was pounding so hard when he woke up he couldn't remember it. He could barely remember his name.

Rakehell went upstairs and swallowed a handful of aspirin and a two-liter of spring water. While he drank the spring water he walked around his house, making sure the prepubescents and Mrs

Bartleberry had unloaded the SUV and put everything back where it was supposed to be. Along the way he stubbed his toe on the corpse of Yicfung. No doubt his wife had purposely left the corpse in the hallway for him to stub his toe on. "Ouch!" he yelped, dropping the spring water. The glass butt of the bottle landed on Yicfung's anemic, bug-eyed face and left a little dent in his forehead.

*

Mrs Bartleberry stepped out of the closet she had been hiding in. "I hope you're proud of yourself." She adjusted the tight plaid apron that accentuated her tight hourglass figure, a figure she maintained without regular exercise despite how many times she had given birth. "That's another prepubescent down the drain. Now pick that dead thing up and take it out back. While you're digging a hole, I'll go upstairs and round up the other prepubescents. The ones that are *alive*."

The Bartleberry's back yard was a cemetery in which twenty-two of the Bartleberry's prepubescents had, after their untimely deaths, been planted. All of them had been killed by freak accidents that usually involved something (a suitcase, an anvil, a safe, a wild turkey, a hostage, etc.) being thrown out of an airplane passing overhead and falling on them; the rest had died of either heart disease or tuberculosis. Twenty-two little gravestones stuck straight out of the cemetery's green, handsomely groomed grass in four rows of five and one row of two, and as Rakehell dug a hole for Yicfung, he flexed his jaw and muttered obscenities, partly because Yicfung was gone, partly because he wasn't in the mood for manual labor, partly because he was hung over—mostly because he was angry at the glacier.

Once Rakehell had finished digging, he cradled Yicfung's body with one of his feet and swept it into the hole. Mrs Bartleberry and the prepubescents, the majority of them straight-faced (Gregious and Furter's faces fidgeted impatiently), were standing around the hole in a half circle. "This never would've happened if that goddamned glacier hadn't come along," panted Rakehell. "I'm gonna teach that damned thing a lesson, me. I'm not kidding."

Rakehell caught Mrs Bartleberry rolling her eyes. "You dare doubt me?" he spat, pointing an index finger at his wife when he said "You" and a thumb at himself when he said "me". Mrs Bartleberry puffed out her lips. The prepubescents, seeing their mother's lips, copied her.

*

Infuriated, Rakehell accused his family of hating him and told them to go inside. Everyone obeyed except for Gregious and Furter: they wanted to play hide-and-seek in the cemetery. But when Rakehell growled at them they obeyed, too. Alone with his thoughts, he passed out, woke up, buried Yicfung, erected a gravestone, and laid a piece of fresh sod down on the newly unearthed patch of dirt in front of it.

After saying a little prayer in Yicfung's name, Rakehell speed-walked to his garage and got an axe.

He ran across his front yard towards the glacier like an Indian running into battle, the axe poised over his head, a war cry ripping out of his mouth . . . He fell on the glacier. He hacked and hacked and hacked on it, his war cry evolving into a series of guttural squawks that sounded something like a heated conversation between two Neanderthals.

The glacier wouldn't break. It wouldn't even chip. But Rakehell was determined to make his mark and he continued to hack away until the head of the axe broke off, flew through his front window and slammed blade-first into the forehead of Bartleberry Bartleberry, the youngest of the prepubescents and by far Rakehell's favorite. Rakehell passed out when the axe head came off, when he found out Bartleberry was dead, and when he was burying Bartleberry in the back yard.

After saying a little prayer in Bartleberry's name, Rakehell speed-walked to his garage and, this time, got a piledriver.

*

"I'll teach you not to gleam with moisture on a hot day!" Rakehell began to fumble with the piledriver's controls. He imagined the thrill of reducing the glacier to a bunch of ice cubes, the whole damned glacier, which was about to get a little taste of his wrath . . . if only he could figure out how to start the piledriver. But there was no start button on the thing. No rip cord either. And it had been so long since

he had used the piledriver . . . When *was* the last time he used it? Had
he ever used it? Why on earth did he own a piledriver anyway? He
couldn't remember. Was the piledriver even his? Maybe he borrowed
it from one of the neighbours. But whoever it belonged to, he couldn't
get the sonuvabitch going, so he bench pressed all 150 lbs. of it over
his head—he was a runty thing and only weighed 150 lbs. himself
but there was so much adrenaline pumping through his system he
threw it up over his head like a ragdoll—and, with a barbaric yawp,
dropped it right in the middle of the piece of the glacier that was
laying on his yard.

The piledriver shattered into a million pieces of steel. A few of
the larger pieces lodged themselves in Rakehell's flesh and his eyes
immediately watered up. He staggered to and fro, punching out at the
air and making dog noises, and as he staggered-punched-barked, he
noticed his next door neighbour, Humidor Humphrey . . .

Humidor was busy trimming his already perfectly sculpted
hedges—compared to Rakehell's not imperfectly (but not perfectly)
sculpted hedges—with a toenail clippers, but he had been watching Rakehell's battle with the glacier out of his eye corners all along.
When Rakehell saw him he tried his best to pretend that he didn't see
him. Humidor saw that he saw him, though, and Rakehell saw that
Humidor saw that he saw him, so he pretended like he hadn't been
pretending not to see him and like there wasn't a glacier in his yard
and he wasn't bleeding from multiple wounds and in more pain than
Mrs Bartleberry when she gave birth to their first, late child, Giddyap
Bartleberry.

Rakehell said, "Hello."

"Hi neighbour," tweeted Humidor with a pinky finger salute.
"Nice day today, dontcha think?" Then, nodding at the glacier: "I like
what you've done with your yard."

*

The ensuing huff from Humidor's nose and shit-eating grin on Humidor's face prompted Rakehell's eyes to roll back into his head and his
knees to buckle. A few seconds later he was curled up like a fetus on
the ground, bleeding, unconscious, and sucking on his thumb. He
remained this way for a long time, his dream-world oscillating back

and forth between a space-time subject to the glacier's tyranny and a space-time that had never known the glacier at all.

Rakehell woke up. The glacier was laying on his legs, waist and halfway up his chest. His arms were loose but no matter how hard he pushed on the glacier he couldn't get it off him. He called to Mrs Bartleberry and the prepubescents, even to his neighbours, but nobody heard him: they were all taking naps and dreaming about flying like trapeze artists over the heads of giant, cheering crowds.

SISTER RUTH

by STEPHEN A. VICINANZA

Tracy heard bayou voices, distant threats and cursing, masked by the sounds of exotic night. She dragged herself up a swampy verge, a long line of vine vegetation hanging from her tired shoulders. She pulled it off as she took a step out into the clearing, sinking to the ankles in soft ground. She gazed downward in bewildered disbelief at the once rustic comfort of expensive outdoor clothing sopped and ragged, the boots hidden in the grass as if she had no feet. She pulled herself free, staring at the small house raised on posts. The ground made obscene sucking noises at her retreat.

She gazed back at yellow-lighted windows with crescent shaped curtains held behind glass panes where condensation offered a romantic fuzz. A storm of insects at each window drawn to the warmth and comfort of the yellow glow there. The house couldn't be more then a hundred feet away, across the marsh grass. It might as well be miles. Her breath ragged, close to exhaustion she put one hand out to lean on the twisted braid of some gnarled tree. It was taller then her but not tall by tree standards, it spread its drooping canopy a scant few feet over her head. The really big trees, the ones that looked like their roots were entwined in a lover's embrace were closer to the water. Tracy swiped at the flying insects before her face. She wanted to sit down and think things over, consider events, find reasonable answers to fearsome questions. She wanted a dry path to the shack up on poles, she wanted . . .

Immediately she came bolt upright. She was astounded to find that she had been falling asleep.

No! That's what Todd did!

The thought brought her to full awareness. One second, that's all it took. One unguarded moment, and just like the others, he'd been gone. She hadn't seen him do it, but she could guess what happened. Tired, wet, frustrated at the lack of reasons for what was happening, he'd slumped down against a tree, while she squatted in the dense growth just feet away.

I was only turned away for a couple of seconds.

Lost, they had been lost trying to get back to the truck. Two days, and finally she'd had to pee.

Maybe I was longer then a couple of seconds.

She hadn't been, and she knew it. Todd had been dead when she turned around. He'd been staring down at a credit card, slipped in high between pressed fingers, as if he'd been praying to the piece of plastic. An icon of false safety, the plastic God.

The guide, Roger Gulden, had carried a portable credit card scanner. He'd carried a bunch of electronic devices, as had everyone. There had been laptops, cell phones, palmtops and hand-held's, GPS tracking equipment, and a mobile radio transmitter. She remembered it all. Cooking gear and stoves, rafts and air pumps, small neat generators, rescue equipment in a special backpack carried by an emergency room doctor. Provisions that could have fed a royal family. None of it remained, none.

Where is it all?

She slid down the strange tree, squatting on humped roots. She hung her head, intending to fall asleep. Two days and nights, lost, without hope of finding a way out of the bayou and she was a hundred steps from safety.

"Is someone out there?"

The words were indistinguishable from the exotic background noise for a few seconds. She thought it was just her own mind picking out what she wanted from the layers of sound.

"Is there someone there? You must speak, I can't see you."

A woman's voice, stern, reserved, that held tones of confidence and something else. Something that sounded wise and sagacious.

Tracy lifted her head.

There was a small deck on the side of the shack. Someone had opened a door there and now stood on the deck holding a lantern. Insects gathered in the sudden brightness.

"If someone is out there, you must speak up. I must get back inside, the bugs are the devil's own this evening."

Tracy rose to her feet, taking a ragged breath. The first sound she had uttered, other then various grunts and moans, in two days. It was merely a high-pitched croak. It was the sound of desperation and caught the woman as she turned to go back inside.

"I can't get to you."

The woman stopped, cocking her head in an odd manner. An exaggerated tilt of the head, lifting one ear to the sounds of the night. "Did someone say something?"

Tracy cleared her throat, quickly. "I can't cross the grass, it's too soft." She was trembling in near panic. What if the woman refused to give her assistance? Was there another house she could go too? Would she give her directions?

The figure turned back to the railing, still listening. "I hear you now. Of course you can't cross, it's swamp grass. What do you want?"

"I'm lost, I need help."

The figure seemed to consider, the silhouette standing quite still, almost unnaturally so. "There are many lost souls in the world. What makes your plight different?" The figure held the lantern out over the deck, scanning the area.

"I'm here, at the edge of the clearing"

The lantern swung around, "And so, what is your special circumstance."

"I was with a tour guide, camping in the bayou. I lost them," she lied. There was some religious overtones to what the woman was saying that warned Tracy to be wary.

"Ahh," came a disgusted reply. "The bayou is for the bugs and snakes, not suburban relaxation. Forgive me, Lord, you weren't with that fool Gulden, were you?"

"Yes," Tracy said excited that the woman had mentioned someone she knew. "Yes, I was with Roger Gulden."

"No wonder you're lost. You're lucky to be alive, at all."

"I'm stuck at the edge of the clearing."

"You just head toward the higher ground, just at the edge of the grass, either side. That'll get you to me."

Tracy moved toward the verge of the grass finding the ground rose higher along the edge. It was still a mass of tangled vegetation but the light of the house gave her a beacon to follow. Presently she arrived at the stairs and climbed these to the deck.

Her first sight of her saviour was through squinting eyes. The woman held the lantern high, its corona, mingling with the halo of the open door, threw the form into deepest shadow. The head was held high, lending authority to a strong voice.

"Who are you, child?"

Tracy looked down at her feet, feeling suddenly humbled by her circumstances. "Tracy Hargrove."

"Just the two names?"

"Tracy Dewitt-Hargrove, I thought it would be easier with just Hargrove."

"Lord forgive me, but most of you have long drawn out names with no meaning behind them. Can't decide who you are, that's what I say. Spoiled, most of you. To much time to ponder yourselves. Praise the Lord. Propriety first, I am Jasmine Defluer, Sister Jasmine will do."

Tracy understood that she was from an intellectual community, who valued their ability to travel and see things others couldn't. She remained silent, knowing the woman wouldn't understand her.

"This fool, Gulden," the shadow continued, "What has become of him?"

"I don't know?" That, at least in part, was the truth.

The head, still tilted high, seemed to scan the air in slow passes. "Things in the bayou should be left to themselves, as Sister Ruth said so many times. Godless, it is, out there, beyond the fens. Come forward, girl, where I can touch you. The Lord has taken my sight these last ten years."

Tracy finally understood why the woman's head was tilted back and she seemed to be slowly scanning everything. The woman was blind.

"Bless the Lord, child, but you sound exhausted."

Sound?

What did exhaustion sound like? She wasn't panting, at least not that she could tell. Her every sense was ignited by fear, tipped to almost hysterical proportions by what happened. She was most likely in shock, and in need of some medical attention. Exhaustion would have to wait, she was too busy to be exhausted.

"Can you help me?"

"Can God help any of us in our folly?"

They stood a long moment, silent, listening to the hum of insects.

"Let me touch your face, child, then we'll see."

Tracy allowed the woman to touch her face, with cool hands. After, they stood again in silence. The woman nodded, as if answering some unspoken question, turning her face to the bayou. It was a gesture with deliberate motions, as if the woman could see something beyond the dense morass and vegetation.

"The bayou likes to keep its secrets."

Cryptic nonsense, Tracy thought at once, swatting unsuccessfully at biting insects on her neck, face and hands. As long as she lets me stay until morning, that's all that matters. It was obviously safe here, or the woman wouldn't be living here alone. In the morning, with directions (the woman must shop, or need to go to a town for something) she could find her way out to the police. They'll find who had killed the others.

"You may stay the night."

Abruptly she turned and entered the house, Tracy, relieved followed the woman inside, shutting the door tightly. After a quick search of the door she found the deadbolt and locked it.

"This the Lord's house, girl." Tracy spun around. "Nothing evil can touch you here."

Tracy didn't want the old woman suspicious or worried. "Force of habit, from the city."

"You're far from the city."

In the brighter light of the interior Tracy could see now the clouded orbs that were the woman's useless organs of sight. The pupils suspended as if in thick fog were blue. As many blind people do, the woman stood with her head tilted slightly back, defiant, secure in her safety.

"I know I am," Tracy said.

"Good, we'll have no more of that, then, shall we, sister." The woman nodded, and turned, walking toward the back of the small house. "You'll stay in Sister Ruth's room, she'd like that, it's fitting."

Tracy picked up her pack where she left it by the door and followed the woman to a small room, sparsely furnished. A thin bed, a nightstand with lamp and bible, a window, one cross above the headboard of the bed.

A cell, she thought.

She put her bag on the bed, then sat, feeling the release of tension flow out through her body. Sister Jasmine stood haughtily at the door, her head tilted back. "There is a town, not far from here."

Tracy looked up, drawing in breath.

"I see, this is important, the town. Tell me, what is your plight? Did you get separated from the others in your foolish band?"

"Yes," Tracy said immediately, feeling this wasn't the time or place to explain herself. She would explain to the police, in the morning.

Sister Jasmine seemed a nice old woman, if a bit overtly religious. No sense in worrying her needlessly, upsetting a woman who already had a handicap. Tracy watched the tall, stout figure carefully, as she nodded to herself.

"All is as it should be, cher," she said, then left the room.

Tracy sat for a long time, listening to the woman busy herself in the small kitchen she had seen when she came in. She was softly singing to herself, a hymn Tracy didn't recognise. Not that she would recognise any hymns, having never been to church for any extended period of time.

When sister Jasmine called Tracy out to eat, Tracy noticed the woman as a whole, complete person for the first time. She was tall with stout shoulders and a substantial neck that held a nearly oval head. She presented a hawkish face that was probably of the Creole set in New Orleans, but not completely French, there was something else there.

She had long straight hair that had greyed to a steely silver with long streaks of black caught-up in a simple ponytail. She was of course blind, but as she spoke of the Lords wishes, according to Sister Ruth, who Tracy thought might arrive at any moment and displace her, either that or the woman was dead, Tracy noticed the movement of her facial muscles exaggerating emotion on an otherwise stony facade.

When she smiled, she revealed a squared mouth full of shining teeth. Tracy, far beyond exhaustion, wrote off her sudden discomfort as being shock.

The thought of Todd brought a sharp pang to her stomach and all at once she had to dash to the bathroom. When she was finished Sister Jasmine had sat down before the fireplace, and Tracy quietly went to her room to cry.

In the night the chill fog descended on the bayou, and Tracy dashed as fast as she could to beat it, because inside the fog something lurked, something cold and wet, something huge and fast as a water snake. It was coming for her, silently, inside the fog and she had to keep ahead of it or it would overwhelm her with blinding speed. But she was tired, bone tired, and just wanted to sleep, against a tree trunk. She couldn't believe what she was doing, sliding out her credit card, and offering it to Gulden who waited beside her with his hand outstretched to the piece of plastic.

"You'll never regret this trip." He was covered in slime and moss, and a large snake flowed about him. Todd walked up and smiled, leaking black slime from his mouth.

Tracy screamed, not because of Gulden and Todd, or the thing that pursued her, but because she was holding the credit card as if praying to it. She sat up in the bed, knowing the dream held somewhat to the tenants of reality. She never expected to dream, nor even sleep, until she was back in civilisation.

The sun was shining and she could hear sister Jasmine moving around the house singing her hymns. It was a stern voice, secure in its confidence.

She heard the knock on the front door and happily, excitedly grabbed her pack and opened the door, just as sister Jasmine's voice came from the area around the front door. "Praise the Lord, it's Sister Ruth, praise be to God, back safely."

Tracy flung open the door, to greet her rescuers. She had time to see the great humped back, a rack of ridges running down in knobs like the dulled tusks of a rhinoceros. The long arms knotted with alien muscle, and the trailing whips of fog at the hands. This was the last she saw, for when it turned its unspeakable swamp face on her, in startled surprise, it was speaking to Sister Jasmine about its joyous return. It had a perfectly ordinary voice.

"Now you must stay, Sister Ruth, and meet our guest." Was the last

thing Tracy heard as the fog whipped around her, freezing her, pulling her down into its milky maw.

YOURS FOREVER

by MARK ZIRBEL

Kyle thought he had taken every precaution.

Whenever he went out with Angie, he made sure it was on a weeknight. Whatever plans they made, he arranged for them to drive separately. When they went out for dinner, he split the bill; when they went to the movies, he bought his own ticket.

Kyle saw to it that theirs was the epitome of a platonic relationship.

Until that July evening . . . sounds of a distant calliope swirling in the river breeze . . . lights from the city dancing in the water as Kyle and Angie walked alongside. And then their hands bumped and their eyes met and in an instant, Kyle realized that he had been kidding himself for months.

That's when he knew.

It was time to call Susan and ask her to give it back.

*

Kyle called in the middle of the afternoon, knowing that Susan would be at work and he would get her machine. It was easier that way, but still not easy.

"Hi, Susan . . . this is Kyle. Look, please listen to this message, okay? This isn't another plea for you to take me back. It's over and I accept that now. As a matter of fact I've met someone new, which kind of brings me to why I'm calling. Umm . . . well, you have something that I'd like to give her. I think you know what I mean . . . Look, Susan, this is really awkward and I'm really sorry, but maybe we could just talk and come to some kind of agreement? Anyway, please call me back or at least leave a message, okay? Umm . . . talk to you soon. Goodbye."

*

A week passed and no word from Susan. In the meantime, Angie invited Kyle to be her guest at an out-of-town wedding reception. It was a month off, but Kyle could already picture Angie out on the dance floor: kicking off her heels (cute polished toes peeking through nylons) . . . glistening with hundreds of mirror-ball freckles . . . leaning in for a sweet rum-and-coke kiss.

Damn, Kyle needed to speak with Susan . . . *and fast.*

*

After two weeks, Susan finally left a message (she left it while Kyle was at work, probably to ensure that she would get his machine): "It's Susan. You can stop by Tuesday evening at six-thirty. I'll be leaving for aerobics at seven, so don't be late."

That was all. There was no discernable tone to her voice—no sense that she was either glad to hear from him or irritated with the intrusion.

Nothing but the words themselves.

Susan invited him in. Kyle sat on the couch—the couch where he and Susan had talked and laughed and slept and ate and touched. Susan brought in a chair from the dining room table and sat across from Kyle. Kyle wasn't sure how to begin, but Susan's *"the clock is ticking . . ."* expression told him he'd best get right to the point. "So . . . do you still have it?" Kyle asked.

"Well, it is mine, isn't it?" replied Susan. "I mean, I didn't ask you to give it to me, but you did."

"Where is it?"

"The basement."

"*The basement?* Are you fucking joking?"

"What am I supposed to do with it, Kyle? Huh? Why don't you tell me!"

"Can I see it?" Kyle asked.

Susan gestured toward the cellar door.

Kyle walked toward the dank, sump-pump corner of the basement. Toward the stacks of boxes filled with old clothes, childhood toys, useless knick-knacks. And then Kyle saw it, nestled between the discarded pieces of Susan's life, lying there on the cold, spider-webbed floor.

It was barely recognizable.

The features of its face had shriveled away, replaced by a giant, spasming vagina. The vaginal lips opened wide, revealing two rows of huge, serrated teeth. Kyle heard gurgling and mewling from within, but the lips snapped shut before he could get a closer look. Kyle shifted his attention to the surface of its torso: dozens and dozens of bright-red penises had erupted through crusty black flesh. The penises twitched and flopped like a den of snakes, dribbling out semen that sizzled and burned against its body.

Kyle knelt down beside it. One of the penises sprang to erect attention, then bent its head in Kyle's direction, scoping him out.

"Hey," said Kyle, "it's been awhile, huh? What do you say I get you out of here? Try and get you back to your old self? I've got a friend that might be able to help. Well, she's more than a friend, actually. Would you like to meet her?"

In one quick motion, the penis reared back, jerked forward, and ejaculated a venomous glob. It splattered against Kyle's arm with an acidic hiss.

"Son of a bitch!" Kyle shouted, springing to his feet.

The thing tried to advance on Kyle, tried to push itself up with decrepit, stick-figure limbs, but it could only raise its frame an inch or two—just enough for some cockroaches to scuttle out from underneath. It collapsed back into atrophied heap.

Kyle retreated upstairs, with the sounds of the thing chittering mindlessly behind him.

"How could you do that to it?" Kyle asked, applying some salve to his arm.

"Please, Kyle," replied Susan, "I'm not in the mood. Go ahead and take it back. Give it to what's-her-name and—"

"Angie!" Kyle snapped. "Her name is Angie."

"Fine. Give it to Angie. Maybe she can nurse it back to health. That is, if she doesn't dump you at the very sight of it."

After all the pain Susan had caused him, she still had the capacity to inflict some more. God, how Kyle would like to give some back. Slap her . . . spit in her face . . . something. But he couldn't. Because he knew that as hideous as the thing in the basement had become, Susan was the only reason that it was still breathing. Not that she was doing anything to care for it. But somehow, just being near her was enough to keep it alive. Surely it wouldn't last a day if taken from her entirely.

Kyle walked toward the front door.

"So what's your decision?" Susan called out.

"Keep it. Like you said, it's yours. I gave it to you unconditionally. I told you it was yours forever. It still is."

Kyle called Angie later that evening. He told her it would be best if they didn't see each other any more.

EXPERIENCE IS THE BEST TEACHER

by JANE GWALTNEY

It wasn't working . . .

She scowled at her reflection. The "frown lines" deepened. "Worry lines" began to appear—She looked away and applied the brake so fast, her head jerked. "Ow," she moaned, rubbing her neck. It crackled, the vertebrae reluctantly aligning. She pushed her sunglasses back in place.

"Hey, babe." His Corvette rumbled, deep-pitched and sexy. Like his voice.

Her fingertips tapped the steering wheel impatiently, as she waited out the red light. "Got somethin' for you. Over *here*!"

It would be foolish to look. She knew better. But still . . . *maybe* . . . She glanced his way, just as the light turned green.

He was pointing at his crotch—

"Aw, grow up!" she yelled. Her tires grabbed the pavement, and she lost him at the next corner.

By the time she'd slowed enough to pull over, her panting had quieted somewhat, but her heart was hammering. She dabbed perspiration from her face and throat and tugged at the neckline of her blouse, using the material as a fan to cool her chest. *Was this some kind of joke? Get rid of the PMS, and hot flashes take its place?* She rifled through her backpack for the cell phone . . .

"Oh . . . I thought you were out, mom. Was just going to leave a message . . . No— I can only come by and get my stuff. Uh, I'm almost to the driveway now. See you in a minute, OK? Bye."

She winced. Mom was standing in the front doorway . . . She parked, slightly askew, and bolted toward the house, head down.

"Jessy, I just don't understand—"

"Let's talk inside," she said, brushing past. *Ahh, the lights were mercifully dimmed. She walked briskly to her room . . .*

The suitcase was filling, and Jessy had so far managed to keep her back turned. "It's just *time*, that's all. Living on campus prepared me for that next step—"

"But, what's the hurry? It's what your *father* said about being 'inexperienced and immature', isn't it? You know he didn't mean it the way it sounded. This isn't necessary," mom dithered.

Forgetting, Jessy spun around. "It's not just dad! *Derek* called me an infantile brat when he cancelled the marriage . . . and-and I don't feel respected *anywhere*. Friends *and* strangers treat me like some sort of object. A *thing*, not an adult—"

"Did Derek hit you?" Mom advanced, and Jessy recoiled, shielding her sunglasses. *Remembering . . .*

"Do you have a black eye under those glasses?" mom demanded.

"No— of course not. Derek . . . Well, he's a *vegetarian*, for Pete's sake!" The packing resumed. "I've been a little weepy, that's all. So my eyes are puffy. Sensitive to light—"

"You taking drugs?"

"*No!* "

"Jessy, this is your home. You didn't need to rent a room. It's as if you're hiding from us . . . and you must do a *lot* of crying. Your voice is deep and husky— A mother *notices* these things."

Jessy sighed and closed the suitcase. "It won't be long. I . . . have to see this through. I'll keep in touch, and we'll get together before classes start again."

Mom was beginning to snuffle as they made their way to the front door. Jessy relented and gave her a quick hug. "This may be the best decision I've ever made. Trust me, mom."

"Gosh . . ." Mom choked on a sob. "You've put on a bit of padding around the middle. You didn't pick up that 'Bulimia' stuff at college, *did you?*"

Jessy's eyes rolled, and she exited, shaking her head and patting her pocket for the keys . . .

"Oh, my *God!* Could you be pregnant?"

Jessy stiffened, then hurled herself into the front seat. "Cafeteria food!" she shouted out the window. The tires squealed, and she was free.

Yes. She could recall the exact moment she had started to hate her voluptuous figure. *Eighth Grade* . . . Billy Crawford's low whistle. *Nice tits,* he'd said— How her face had burned.

She held the dangling price tag off her nose and blinked, bringing the eye chart into focus. She double checked the numbered empty space on the rack. +1.75 *Intermediate* . . . She snatched off the glasses and looked for the matching numbers on the temple. Finding only a blur, she growled and plucked a second pair from the rack, using it to read the numbers on the first.

Satisfied, she gathered her additional purchases and deposited them on the pharmacy counter. She leaned forward, peering expectantly into vacant air—

A nearby clattering progressed swiftly to the unmistakable sounds of spilled and rolling pills. After a momentary scuffling, an enthused young man swaggered up to the cash register. "And what'll it be, today?" he beamed.

"Um, do you have any of those herbal supplement things for . . ." She cleared her throat, nervously. "Hot flashes. You know . . . uh, for—"

"So your mother's got you doin' her shopping, eh?" He winked. "Yeah, we carry several brands. "They don't do my mom any good, though. 'Bitchy' ain't the word for it—"

"Pardon me?" Jessy feared she would hyperventilate. The sudden flush of warmth was a major nuisance. But the overwhelming surge of rabid lust was just plain terrifying. "Check me out, please— I—I'm in a hurry!"

The machine whirred and pinged. "I'm checkin' you out, alright," the pharmacist laughed. "Oh, *sorry.* Bad joke." *His eyes were devouring her . . .*

She was flustered, desperate . . . The key turned, at last! She darted inside and closed out the world.

This wasn't making sense. She sank into the welcoming recliner. *She was changing, at a dizzying pace . . . had matured at least twenty-five years since mid-night—* "Some enlightenment. People are *still* treating me like an empty headed bimbo!" *Surely she was entitled to a refund. She'd take that con artist to* court— Her shoulders hunched. "Yeah *right*, Jessy." She picked up the remote. "Talk about airheads. What judge would believe *this*?"

The late afternoon talk shows were spinning their webs. Her attention span waning on the subject of juvenile prison reform, she flipped to the next channel . . . Her jaw dropped. The topic was "Mid-Life Madness: The Multi Orgasmic Woman". A pack of paunchy ex-husbands was expressing outrage at being abandoned in favour of "young studs".

Jessy leapt from her chair and paced, but the room was too compact to dilute her restless cravings. She needed chocolate, and she needed sex— She needed them *now*! The phone was giving her a "come hither" look . . . The next thing she knew, she had called Derek.

"Yes, you heard me right," she emphasised. "I realise what you said is true. *All* of it, especially about sex. There wasn't enough, and I was too inhibited. I nee— er, *we* needed less talking and more sex . . . *Sure*, I want to see you! Let me give you directions here . . . Oh, and Derek? Bring me a one pound box of chocolate truffles, OK?"

The adrenaline rush made her feel downright frisky. After converting the futon frame to "bed status", she donned the silk robe Derek had bought her. But her dash to the bathroom delivered a jolt of reality— She froze in front of the mirror, comb in hand, and stared in horror at the silver streaking her hair like a road map . . .

The door opened, barely more than a crack.

"Jessy? Wow, it's dark in— *Hey!*"

Jessy yanked him through the widened crack. She slammed the door, then grabbed his shoulders, turning him to face it.

"What the—"

"Shut up, Derek. You're *mine*, now," she whispered, slipping a blindfold over his eyes. "Give me that candy and behave, or I'll have to hurt you!"

" . . .*Damn*," he shivered.

No cussin' without permission," she warned. Shredding the wrapper, she ripped it from the package and dove in. She proceeded to ravish the truffles and Derek simultaneously, shoving both him and the empty box back into the hall approximately one hour later . . .

"Run along, baby," she said, setting her alarm clock. "I'm refreshingly free of the need to discuss marriage plans. You keep banging on my door, and a guy with a badge'll escort you home."

Derek's pitiful whimpering persisted. "I love you more than ever . . . I want to give you babies and grow old with you, Jessy!"

Wonder and poignant joy threaded her veins, nearly stilling her heart. She ran into the bathroom and flipped the wall switch, flooding the interior with light. The mirror registered her anguish, then her determination. *She had to know . . .*

"Come back in, Derek. When I turn on the lamp, take a good look. But first, listen carefully. I need to ask you some questions. Your answers are vital."

He took her in his arms, but she gently pushed him away. "First of all, would it *matter* if I can't have babies?"

His instant reply was startling. "Of course not, honey. You're *more* than enough."

She fumbled in semi-darkness, until her fingers found the pull-chain. "Am I?" she asked, as she sat down and bathed her face in the Tiffany's glow. "I've grown up a *lot* since I last saw you, haven't I? I'm on my way to growing 'old' already—"

"You're beautiful! How could you ever be anything *but?*" He was running his hands through her hair . . .

The details about yesterday's events could wait.

Pain was inching up her spine and sending satellite signals throughout her body. She rolled stiffly onto her side, groaning aloud with the effort.

Derek stirred, but didn't awaken. A sunbeam highlighted his nakedness, skipping and playing across his firmly defined contours. Jessy's misery receded as her eyes fixed on the abundance of his hair tickling the pillowcase . . . As always, jet black stubble awaited his morning shave. Out of habit, she reached, anticipating the nubby delight against her fingertips—

Her scream was hoarse, her shock equalling *nothing* yet experienced during her entire lifetime. Her *short* lifetime—

"Huh?" Derek's eyes flew open, and he jerked upright.

"Don't look at me!" Jessy ordered. She pitched forward and scrambled unsteadily to the bathroom, slamming the door behind her.

Her hands were misshapen claws, and their shrivelled crepe-like covering extended to include the rest of her. *The skin of a woman of eighty.* The room spun as she raised her face to the mirror . . .

She could tell she was in Derek's arms again, but even after several blinks, he remained fuzzy. The futon frame creaked—

"Jessy! Should I take you to an emergency room?"

"No . . . *please*. There's nothing they can do. Only *Ulalume* can help me. Take me to her. N-not sure I can drive . . . I think I'm getting cataracts."

"Who? *Cataracts*? Don't be silly. Now, I *know* you hit your head—"

"Don't you want to know how I got like this? So *old* and sick and ugly . . ." She began to weep, mournfully. "How can you stand to look at me?"

Derek shrugged. "You don't look any different."

"Why are you being so cruel? At least be *honest* with me!" she beseeched. "I'm only twenty-one, and I'm bent like a pretzel—"

He cut her off with his laughter. "Age is a state of mind, Jessy. I know that's a cliché, but . . . Well, you've *always* been pre-occupied with your looks. So pre-occupied, you can't see that I'm *not*. That's what our split was about. Your lack of trust. If you were grossly dis-figured tomorrow, you'd still be the person I've shared my dreams with— The one who never stops looking for answers. You'd still be *you*."

She cringed in agony, as he gave her an encouraging squeeze. "You just need to convince *yourself*," he finished.

Rapture . . . Her sniffling stopped. "Maybe my latest search for answers has done just that. Oh, how I love you, Derek!"

"Yes!" he exalted. Let's make love all day." He clasped her body to his, in a frenzy of passion.

"*What?*" she gasped. "You're kidding— I can barely *move*!"

Derek made a sour face and rolled off her. "So . . . *still* withholding sex every time we have a silly argument."

"Argument? Don't you get it? I have to get to Ulalume! My hair's grey, and I'll probably be bald by—"

"*Hello?* You discovered a grey hair? Is *that* what all this is about? I thought you'd wised up, but no—Melodramatic, as ever." He had put on his pants and was slipping his T-shirt over his head. "Speaking of which, first thing in the morning, you scare the crap out of me with some God-awful shrieking. What a way to wake up! Was that some kinda' *re-birthing* shit? The marriage is off— *Again!*"

If only she could muster the energy to throw him out properly . . . She pointed a crooked finger at the door. "Go," she croaked feebly.

She squinted at the windshield, worming her way through traffic. *People in a hurry.*

An elderly woman pulled up beside her. "Brand new driver?" she asked, sweetly. "Don't let the horns get to you." Giving a "thumbs up", she sailed on by . . .

Ulalume's Antique Shop awaited. Jessy had located the parking lot she knew to be closest, a one block walk. Her hands trembling, she tried repeatedly to lock up the car, but the keyhole eluded. She bent, her lower back throbbing, and searched with her fingertips.

"Hey . . . Nice ass."

The voice was close-by. She halfway straightened, leaning against the car for support, and turned.

The young man whistled, almost inaudibly. "Nice tits, too," he added as he drove away.

Jessy sighed, then wheezed. "My God, it's true! Men'll screw any-thing." She hobbled off . . .

She appeared exactly as before, materialising before Jessy's eyes . . . in the plush velvet wing-back chair. "You return to Ulalume, as I knew you would." She bowed her head, slightly. "But, then . . . I am The Seer."

"Well, I'm *not,* Jessy snarled. "And I'm not ready to be one of your antiques, either. Wisdom— *Bah!* You know what I learned? People lie, that's what. I already *knew* that."

Dingy grey smoke spindled from the ancient hag's "porthole" of a mouth. She leered, like a toothless Jack O' Lantern. "I could have told you that."

"Sure, sure. But I'm young and naïve— Or, I *was,* rather. This sucks! Give me back my youth. I feel like shit, and it's not worth it. 'Pretty and dumb' will do me just fine."

Ulalume leisurely shuffled cards, stopping intermittently to upright several across her lap. "The deck was stacked, and so are you." She presented Jessy with a lewd wink. "You are beginning to see the former, but the latter will remain visible only to others."

Her audience's eyes widened.

"Allow me to make it clearer, Jessica. Your ageing process is seen and felt solely by you. The rest of humankind still perceives you as a beautiful and rather gullible twenty-one year old . . . Oh— with *one* exception. Your mother— Mothers *notice* things." Her craggy eyebrows lifted. "But, *no*. She won't treat you as an adult, *ever*."

A tide of emotions engulfed Jessy, relief on the forefront, and she staggered . . . giddy. An onslaught of delirious laughter left her breathless. "Wow! This has been an awesome experience. I *do* have insight. Thank you, thank you, *thank you*! Knowing what I know now, I can go back and do it right. This is the *wisdom* you promised." She scooted an intricately carved oak chair up close to Ulalume and lowered herself into it. "Ok, I'm ready. Reverse the process."

A flaming corona outlined Ulalume's bulbous head, and sulphur yellow etched her fire-coal orbs. Jessy drew back as an alchemic explosion showered her with sparks, but she was held fast to her seat by anticipation.

Suddenly, all was quiet. Ulalume's coarse features had melted away, and in their place flashed a succession of images.

"It's *me*," Jessy murmured, transfixed. It was as if home movies from consecutive stages of her life had been spliced together for convenient viewing.

With an audible "pop", Ulalume re-appeared. "You wish to go back and do it right, yes? I'm afraid you were right the first time. You were as wise as you will *ever* be when you came to my shop the first time, *and* the second. As you said, *people lie* . .".

She gathered Jessy's hand in her own and gave it a maternal pat. "The process is irreversible, my dear."

THE SHADOW OF A MAN (SEEKING THE CHILD)

by ROBERT N. STEPHENSON

The rain kept falling, harder and harder as if the sky had rent and all the souls of millennia, liquefied, flowed onto the Earth in search of what they had lost. Pools formed around drains as they crowded the exits. They formed puddles on the footpath, a congregation of like souls, and they fell as the single dark drops of the lonely and the lost.

Lightning lit the sky. As a mighty crash shook the world, Mitchell squeezed in tighter under the bus shelter. Thunder roared again, it shook the shelter and his bones; for a moment his heart stopped. In that flash of light he went back. It was red, he was a child and the world was pain.

"Fuck it!" Mitchell cursed as he slammed his fist into the shelter's billboard, knocking a neat hole through the fibro sheeting. The rain came heavier as though the multitude now wept for a long dead God. Gutters, clogged with rubbish, overflowed. He had to stand on the shelter's seat.

The wind gusted, rain sprayed his face and he was cold. Over the drumming on the roof the sound of a cell phone, playing a happy tune, invaded Mitchell's sodden misery. He'd forgotten to turn it off when leaving the office. His body shook and his teeth crushed together as another flash and roar slapped at him, flashed him back then forward again. He caught his breath, sucked in wet air and answered the phone. Business was business.

"Yaeger Property Investments," he answered. He'd been in business exactly thirteen weeks and six days since coming out of hospital. He'd learned a lot of helpful stuff from the team of psychiatrists that helped him through his stay. They helped him rediscover his personality, helped him to leave a lot of stuff behind, though no-one could tell him why he'd been in hospital in the first place, but he knew it had been for a long time.

"You do buildings?" a deep voice asked. "Old buildings?"

Mitchell shivered with the cold. He felt a trickle of water run between his buttocks. "Do you wish to invest in property?" he asked calmly, as a car cruised past and sprayed the shelter. He turned his back to protect the phone.

"I want to buy a building, if that's what you want to know." The voice sounded agitated.

"Certainly, Mr . . .?" He paused and waited for the man to fill in the blank. Silence. "Do you . . .?"

"Darcy," the man said quickly. "Darcy Davis." There was another long pause.

"Now, Mr Davis, what building do you wish to purchase?" Mitchell bit down hard to stop his teeth chattering.

"I can hear water," Darcy said.

"You caught me on my way home, Mr Davis. I'm sheltering out of the rain while waiting . . . " he stopped. "I'm waiting for my chauffer to bring the car around." Darcy was quiet for a moment. Mitchell looked up the street and saw his bus approaching. The smell of damp clothes reminded him of a wet dog. He shivered. "What property were you considering . . . "

"I ain't considering shit!" Darcy screeched. "I want Glenside Asylum!"

"I don't believe that building is on the market, Mr Davis." Mitchell was sure it was heritage listed. Sale would be difficult if it did come on the market. There was something about the voice that bothered him. He couldn't place it, but deep down he felt a pang of anger at its sound.

"You work out the details, I'll throw the money." Mitchell heard heavy breathing on the line. The bus' lights shone through the rain. They showed a shimmering veil of water surrounded by the dullness of night. The bus was almost at his stop. "I want Glenside. I want a yes or a no, Mr Yaeger. Can you do it?"

He considered the request for moment. He needed the money and knew there was always a way around red tape. "Yes," he said. "Call into my office at nine tomorrow and we'll talk more about it."

"I'll be there at nine on the dot, Yaeger. Nine tonight on the steps of Glenside." The phone went dead.

"Bastard!" he yelled. There was only an hour to get to the asylum and he was wet through. The bus pulled up and showered Mitchell in more buckets of garbage littered water.

"You want this bus, mate?" the driver asked, looking at him through the opened door.

"No!" Mitchell yelled, as he kicked the side of the bus.

"Hey! What do you think you're doing?" the driver squealed, and he closed the door and drove off.

Mitchell screamed abuse at the departing bus before walking across the flooded street and back to the office. He kept some casual clothes in a locker for Friday nights down the club. Blood dripped from small cuts on his knuckles. Rain washed the drops pink across his fingers. Breathing deeply he closed his eyes and tried to calm himself.

Another flash, this time it wasn't lightning. Red on red and the sound of singing, a shadow crying and the feeling of something missing; taken away.

He sloshed through the flooded footpaths towards the building, trying to clear his eyes.

A car crawled toward him, its lights a dull yellow. Mitchell turned. A bearded face stared at him through an opened window. Wet and matted. The car stopped. A gun appeared, pointed in his direction. Mitchell threw himself down, the gun barked, thunder roared as the night lit up like a silver shot.

Flash!

Water filled his mouth as he tried to scamper to safety on all fours. Laughter rang out and a car door slammed. Mitchell's heart clogged his throat; he felt heavy, slow; his mind a mess of fear. Water splashed under his hands, he couldn't see, he didn't know which way to go.

"Scared, are we?" screamed the man. "Lucky I missed, eh?"

Mitchell's hands slipped from under him and he fell forward into the overflowing gutter. He rolled onto his back, spluttering. Rain filled his eyes. A dark shadow leaned over him blocking the water's fall.

"You don't remember me do you, Nathan?" A hand grabbed Mitchell by the collar and yanked him to his feet. The sky lit up again. He saw the ugly face grinning at him through a silver night. Teeth missing, nose spread, eyes dark and sunken in his head. Thunder punched him in the chest a few seconds later. The storm was moving away. "Fifteen years dulls your memory some, doesn't it?"

"Hey, I got money . . . "

"Stuff your money, Nathan." The man pressed the short barrelled gun into Mitchell's cheek.

"My name's Mitchell, you got me mixed up with some . . . "

"That what you call yourself now, is it?" Mitchell saw the hammer move back. He closed his eyes. The toothless face filled his mind. It was a victim's face, a dead man's face.

Click.

*

A stinking horse blanket was pulled back, Mitchell's eyes burnt with torchlight. He tried to swallow but the wadded cloth between his teeth sucked his mouth dry. He dry-retched.

"Nathan," a new voice said behind the light. "Welcome back to Glenside." The light flicked off and rough hands pulled him from the back seat of the car. Wet cloth grabbed at his skin. The cold made him numb.

He tried to speak but all he managed was a mumbled reply.

"Nathan French," the new voice said, as he was dragged through the darkness towards a dim light. It was a doorway, ajar. "You're here so we can dish out some long overdue justice. This is what you should've got fifteen years ago, you sick bastard!" A blow to the back of the head brought flashes to his mind, his eyes.

The door creaked then banged shut. Light came from a single bulb, the room smelt dank. The odour of wet cloth and hair filled his nostrils. Mitchell was dumped in the middle of a small room; he shivered with fear as much as cold. He could hear the whispers of voices and the stomping and shuffling of feet. He kept his eyes closed; his mind swirled, small visions flecked his thoughts like rain drops in front of bus lights at night. Blood flowed across his soul, warm, wet and sticky. He shuddered.

Flash!

"What have you been doing all these years, Nathan?" the voice of the man with the gun asked, as he stepped closer, into the light. "Did you think no one would come looking for you? Did you really think you could get away with your butchery?"

Suppression, forced suppression, drugged suppression, fuzzy memories; fuzzy light pushed its blanket over Mitchell. It was warm, comforting. Behind his eyes, in the spotted red light, he laughed at the game, the chase and the prize. Mitchell's eyes snapped open. He stared into the toothless man's face and waited. *Let them come,* he heard a child say. He tried to sit up but he was too numb. He bit into the gag.

A second man stepped into the light. He was small, round and baby-like. His eyes pale, sad and his mouth was a twist of contempt. *Another picture in a paper, a sad, distraught young man, pleading, desperate.* Mitchell shook his head.

"How do you feel, Nathan?" the second man said softly. "Afraid?"

"We should just leave you here and let you freeze to death," laughed the man with the broken smile. He nudged the second. "Hey, it would be slow and painful. Keeps our hands clean, what do you think?"

The round man walked forward and knelt beside Mitchell. "You don't remember anything, do you?"

Mitchell's eyes burned with cold fire. *Skin peeled from muscle, eyes wide with horror.* He shook his head again and remembered the slice of a knife and the screams that never ended.

"Then maybe it is best this way," he said, standing up. "To die without reason is a suitable punishment for the likes of you."

"Ugh!"

Flash!

Mitchell was rolled on his back from the force of the kick, his jaw cracked; pain filled his mind with white sparks. He tasted blood. Wet, warm, sticky blood. *A knife-edge on soft skin flashed before his eyes. Mitchell listened to the slice and the sound of the opening incision and saw the red of muscle and the stained white glow of bone.*

Flash of light. Flash of pain.

Red. Red. Red.

"Die, Nathan, die," someone said as the single bulb burning through his eyelids winked out, and the dancing spots of darkness closed in around him.

"If you're not dead when we come back, we'll see to it you wish you had been."

The door slammed shut, the click of a lock and the growl of a car penetrated him like the bite of the cold. Mitchell clenched his eyes tight and counted the spots behind his lids.

*

"Mr Yaeger?" the wisp of a woman's voice said. "You have a visitor."

Mitchell opened his eyes. The overhead fluorescent lights glowed clean white. He said nothing. The nurse was young, her face pretty. He clenched his fists and willed himself patience. Red on white always took his breath away.

"Mr Yaeger?" a man's voice. Familiar. "I'm Darcy Davies." He watched Mitchell for a moment. "When you didn't show, I walked about the asylum's grounds. I heard groaning from a storage building and broke down the door." The man's voice was smooth, calm and measured. "What happened?"

Darcy Davis was tall, thin, his eyes alive, calculating.

"You're a policeman?" Mitchell said, recognizing the stance and bearing of the man. He knew his face, knew those eyes. Oh how he wanted to hold those eyes. "How long have I been here?"

"A few hours." Darcy looked him hard in the face. "And yes, I'm a detective sergeant from the city station. Now, can you tell me what happened? Why were you bound and left in that room? Did you know your attackers?"

"What do you want, detective?" Mitchell asked. "What was the phone call all about, really?" He knew this man, knew the pain he had caused.

"What I want is some answers," he said, as he grabbed the bedside chair and sat down. Mitchell saw his gun, as his torn leather jacket fell back away from his hip.

"I'm not answering anything without my lawyer present." The

reek of stale cigarettes clashed with the hospital smells. Darcy was a smoker.

Flash. Flash. Red.

Darcy closed his note pad, licked his teeth with his mouth closed, sat back in the chair and sighed. "I'm following you, Nathan," he said softly, "watching your every move."

"Nathan?" Mitchell wasn't surprised but he went along. The name felt right now, comfortable.

"Since your release I've been keeping an eye on you, making sure the treatment they used on you worked. They said you were cured. I . . . "

"What treatment, and what's this with calling me Nathan?" His fists clenched harder, he focussed his energy on the calm, cool water of a bath. Water tinted pink.

Darcy looked at him carefully, as if making an important decision. "I can't tell you much, Mitchell," he said with a heavy sigh. "You were a sick boy a long time ago and some doctors tried a new treatment on you. I didn't think it would work, but . . . "

"I have no idea what you are talking about," Mitchell smiled inside. A new game was afoot.

"I called you last night to see if you'd have any reaction to my name or to the mention of Glenside Asylum." Darcy stood and slid the notebook into his jacket's inside pocket.

"It's a heritage building, I don't think you can buy it," Mitchell said harshly. "Now go away. I've nothing to say to you."

Darcy gave Mitchell a card, bid farewell and left. The nurse came back and took Mitchell's temperature. A food-services woman, in a green uniform, delivered a meal, hidden beneath a thick plastic food warmer. Broiled steak and soft vegetables. He checked the ward and saw that those who were not asleep were carefully eating their bland meals. The bedside locker only had his coat. The draw held his wallet, watch and house keys.

*

No one stopped him as he left the hospital; the nurse's body wouldn't be discovered until someone decided to check the storage cupboard. The main entrance security service was busy helping frantic nurses and doctors with road accident victims. Mitchell caught a taxi home and payed by credit card. He found it hard signing the cardholder's name.

Once inside his small apartment he dove under the shower and let the heat of the water soak deep into his skin, it went all the way to the bone. Closing his eyes he saw the face of the toothless man staring at him through a TV screen, he was pleading, his eyes filled with tears. Nathan had an erection. Excitement filled him, as the water washed down his body in sensuous rivulets. He groaned as his tension abated.

Red. Flash. Red. The shadow unfurled.

Nathan dressed in warm clothes. He didn't like Mitchell's taste too bland; too nice. In the kitchen he searched for something he could eat on the run, and a sharp knife. The fridge was filled with half-eaten TV dinners, a few bottles of beer and a can of fish. He grabbed the can of fish, cut the lid off with an opener, snatched a dirty fork from the sink and headed out the door.

It was early evening; still light enough to walk to Glenside in relative safety. There were too many thugs on Adelaide's streets lately. *Gangs of the unemployed and the unemployable*, Nathan guessed. He didn't like being afraid on the streets, streets should be safe.

It was only two kilometres from the apartment. The old asylum sat low in a gully, protected from view by a stand of eucalypts and low grown shrubs. The garden had been left to go wild over the years and paper rubbish had collected in the bushes' lower branches. Nathan carefully made his way through the main gates, ensuring nobody saw him enter. The road to the building was about a kilometre long. Now half way to the building, Nathan's old confidence was returning. He felt at ease with the plan unfolding in his mind, he wondered if his room still wanted him back. *If they were still there.*

"Hey, you!" called someone from behind him. "Turn around slowly."

Nathan turned and saw a man in security uniform staring at him, his hand on his gun.

"This is private property," he said as he pointed back towards the gate.

Flash!

"You understand me?" the guard said. His face hard, his eyes sharp.

Nathan smiled. "I have an appointment at seven," he said calmly.

"This place has been closed for five years, mister," the guard said.

"But I have a card." Nathan put his hand in his pocket and walked towards the guard. "Please, have a look."

The guard stepped back a pace. "Stay where you are."

Nathan stopped and sighed. "I just flew in from Melbourne. I've been away for the last few years and this was meant to be a check in with my doctor. Doctor Westborne." He took another step closer.

"Give me a look at that card," the guard said, also stepping closer. "All the patients were moved over to St James Hospital five years back, I guess you should . . . "

He fell screaming, blood gushing from his neck. Nathan straddled him and drove the knife through his chest while stuffing the empty fish tin in his mouth. The guard thrashed. Nathan plunged the knife again. Blood covered his hands, soaked into the knees of his trousers. With another plunge the guard lay still. Nathan breathed heavily. Rage had flowed through him like he'd never felt before. "Control, I need control," he sighed. He closed his eyes to think, to focus. He'd never lost it before; it was his artistry, style, to do things calmly, slowly, gently. Nathan opened his eyes and looked down on the bloodied guard's face. He sliced off his ears and put them in his pocket, dragged the body down the slope a little, and rolled it into a thick growth of bushes.

To hear is to be blessed
The sounds of reason
The sounds of laughter
The sounds of death

Nathan recited the little verse he'd just made up, as he fondled the two soft, fleshy rewards in his pocket. He found the broken door at the back of one of the smaller buildings that dotted the park-like grounds. The main asylum stood white, monolithic against the backdrop of trees. Three stories of madness, pain and torture he thought, as he found a window on the third floor he recognized. Built in the fifties it was meant to represent the new era in design, exaggerated cornices, deep-set windows and wide welcoming doors. White paint had peeled in places to show the grey of heartless concrete. He looked about the feral landscape and saw the greenery of eons ago. The neat ordered flowerbeds tended by patients; the grassy slopes for relaxing and reading. His memory of yesterday was pain made new.

He pushed aside the broken door and stood in the little room in which he'd been thrown to die. The light was still on. There was a wet stain on the floor where he had lain on the bare concrete.

Slice, carefully, neatly, slice. Blood flowed from a gash on his forearm. He wrote a message on the floor and signed it with one of the ears.

Room 7 - 3 west. Come hear me sing.

*

Creaking in the darkness, the bed reminded Nathan of leather straps and injections. Night had fallen and he sat on the edge of an old bed frame in the centre of the room. His room, his prison, his home. He stood, paced across the room and punched the wall. The lights came on. One blinking fluorescent tube and a yellow reading light on the wall. The strobe effect matched pace with his breathing. It was peace. It was surreal.

Would they come? he wondered. Yes, they had to. They had the fire of revenge in their hearts. Blood flows hotter when passion is involved.

"Wait for them," a child's voice whispered.

"Leave me the spoils," a dark shadow said, as it played across the walls.

The walls were dirty, stained by time, stained by his hands. He smelt the defecation of rats, the dry dustiness of a room shut for years. In a corner he heard the crying of a man, afraid, tormented. His clothes were stained with sweat and old food, his hair shorn short, his arms locked about him in a forced embrace, a child's age in his heart; in his mind. Wardens taunted. They spat and urinated on his bed.

"I should choke you with your own cock," one squawked like a black crow. "Tie a rock around ya neck and throw you in the river."

"You can eat shit for all we care," another laughed, as he dropped his trousers and shat on his dinner plate.

A child's crying echoed around the room. Screaming, punching, yelling. Doctors streamed about pointing, whispering, nodding and writing notes. Later, he was newly clothed, washed and fed and the bed fresh. The vision a lie. Then pain, great pain. Pain and light, pain and sound, pain and the smell of disinfectant, the smell of sweat and shit and vomit.

Nathan fingered a scrape on one of the walls and knew its life, its role in remembering. He fingered a small scar above his right eye, ran his tongue over a chip in his front tooth. Yesterday revealed its secrets. *He felt the blow of a nurse's fist, his face. His teeth bit into the plaster of the wall, blood and pain. He felt straps, a needle in his arm and a brace around his head. Faces loomed over him, voices; a cacophony of sound smashed against him like waves. Drugs pulsed into his mind; a haze swallowed him, swallowed Nathan. Then came the night, the cold eternity of nothingness. The scrape on the wall bled into his soul. He'd tasted blood back then. He licked his forearm. He tasted blood now.*

"Where are you, you bastard!" screamed a loud voice.

"They've come," he smiled, as he gently ran his fingers down the blade of the knife. *Slice, sweet delicate slice.*

Flash. Red. Flash. The shadow breaths.

"Answer us, you fucking freak!" screamed another voice. He heard them walking carefully down the hallway that led to his room.

Step, pause. Step, pause.

Nathan began tapping the knife on the frame of the bed to the rhythm of his mind. The child laughed and began to sing a song about pulling wings off sparrows.

Tink, tink. Tink, tink

The sound rhythmic, deep, exciting. Lust swelled his heart, his lungs filled, hungry for air. The smell of fear hung on the still air.

"There!" hissed one of them. "The light."

He heard the click of a gun being cocked. He switched off the light. The light of the half moon shone its grey love across the floor, over the wall. He had an erection, his blood pounded in his veins, forced hard against his skin. He turned and faced the window. The silver light played across his face. Nathan drew in a deep breath and felt the moon fill his lungs with decadent dust. He tapped the knife.

Tink, tink. Tink, tink

A blinding flash, an explosion of sound, the spray of plaster and stone.

"Not even close," Nathan said after the ringing had died down.

He found the wall and traced its patterns toward the door. Whispers flooded the darkness; shadows crossed the moonlight. A glint of metal, a scream, the gurgle of letting and the thud of finality came with the beating of his heart.

"Timmon!" A hiss of sound, edged with fear. The pulse grows greater, the flow faster. Nathan adds a finger to his catch. Later he will work.

A stumble, a cry; the striking of metal on concrete, the gun clatters free.

"Your wife was a sweet prize," Nathan says, recalling her smile just before his blade poured out her juices. He circles the body on the floor, sees the glint of the gun in the moonlight. Ecstasy shivers in his muscles, tears well in his eyes; the power is his, the flavour divine. He steps into the moonlight. The moon now behind, he sees the kneeling man. "You will feel everything." He focuses on the building rage. He must hold it, calm it. It must not ruin his work.

The man dived for the gun, Nathan slashed with the knife; the shadow could see. The man screamed and cowered towards the doorway. "I want your tongue to come to me first," Nathan hissed. "Then your eyes."

"Please no, please," cried the man, only his legs were visible in the light.

Nathan steadied himself, the knife wet, sticky in his hand. He drank in the power, his hunger urgent. "You are mine. Scream and I shall love you, cry and I shall hold you, fight and I shall enjoy you."

A flash of light, a crash of sound threw Nathan from his feet. Pain smashed through his shoulder, he dropped the knife, he roared at the moon. The lights flicked on. Darcy stood in the doorway, gun in hand, his eyes flickering to the light. At his feet lay the slashed form of the first man, toothless and oozing. A fork stood erect from one of his eyes, his throat slashed. Beside the door, sitting back against the frame, was the other man. Blood stained the floor around him, his wrist hanging limply.

"I knew you would come," Nathan gasped. He could taste the smoke from the gun. He struggled to his knees. Pain beat in rhythm with the light.

"I knew you hadn't been cured, Nathan." Darcy knelt and checked for a pulse on the prostrate man, he looked to the sitting one. "I found the dead security guard." He stared at Nathan. "His wife called the station when he didn't come home for dinner. Karl's always punctual."

"I hadn't begun my work, as you can see," Nathan slid his left hand into his coat pocket. He felt the blindness on anger building in his gut. He breathed quickly, struggling to hold it down.

"You've become sloppy, Nathan," Darcy said harshly.

"For you I will be calm." Nathan felt the old rush of pleasure as he visualized Darcy opened up before him.

"This time, I'll see you get put down for good, and no children's court will save you now." Darcy pulled a handkerchief from his pocket and handed it to the injured man; his shoulder exploded in blood, the room rang. The smell of burning powder filled the air.

Nathan crawled to his feet, throwing the gun at the now prone Darcy. "You make me sick with your guns!" he screamed, as he lunged at Darcy and kicked him hard in the head. "You . . . fucking . . . weak . . . bastard . . . " he yelled between kicks. He grabbed up the knife and in one quick action slit the throat of the sitting man. Blood sprayed the wall, Nathan kicked the man and he slid sideways to the floor. Darcy opened his eyes and looked up at Nathan.

"No," he whispered. Blood was pouring from his wound, pooling around his head.

"You didn't check to see if the guard still had his gun, did you?" Nathan sat down on Darcy's chest. Darcy grunted under the weight. "Do I look stupid, detective?" Nathan screamed into Darcy's face. Spittle dripped from his lips, he wanted to vomit on the man but it would taint the gift to his inner self. He had to release the rage so he could later savour the slice and the wet, sticky bath. He plunged his good hand into the bullet wound in his shoulder and screamed, howled like a wolf at the moon. The rage left him, fled to leave a sweetness that ached and throbbed with his heart.

"I had to leave them behind. The demons," he leant in close to Darcy. "The darkness. They took them from me, robbed me of my right; my will."

"Please. No!" Darcy cried. He lifted his head but Nathan smashed it back into the floor.

A shadow stepped down from the ceiling and stood behind Nathan. It sucked in the light. It hissed with expectation. "Mine is the life," it wheezed. "Let me suck the breath from his lips."

"Feel the blade, feel the steel, feel the power of my invasion!" Nathan raised the knife. "Feel the anger of a child's loss."

A small child of five stepped out of the near wall. He wore a tattered dressing gown and one red slipper. The boy looked angelic in a homeless kind of way. He stepped up beside Nathan and took the knife. It looked big in his small, delicate hand. Darcy tried again to move but Nathan pushed him hard into the floor.

"This is the child within the man." The child grinned, showing pointed yellow teeth. His eyes turned black.

"No!" Darcy screamed. "Oh God, please no!"

"Listen to the music," Nathan sang, "listen to the sound of dying." The child lunged and the darkness lowered to take the last breath.

THREE REDNECKS AND
AN ANDROID-SHELL

by HERTZAN CHIMERA and M.F. KORN

EPILOGUE

On a TennaCo oil-pipeline planet, Smithers Van Eckhart was throwing up over the rotting iron railing of the rig into the bubbly boily plankton-choked sea.

Tommy Tool Room and The Fatboy were yucking it up so much watching him hanging off the side, a hundred feet above the huge concave green-pea soup, the technicoloured yawn of blue freeze dried crud fell a long way beforebeing swallowed up by the choppy churny briny.

"You okay, Smithers, old fella?" he asked his barfing rigbuddy.

"Fuck you, chip flipping idiots." Smithers Van Eckhart was a real funny colour now, sorta off-purple like the colour of cardial infarction on an old girl's lips, this is in the time before they fitted auto pilot heart-jumpers as standard. In the 'good old days', you hear the really old and scrawny rigbuddies go on about it. The good old days, hacking up an old tar-clogged lung.

Tommy Tool Room always loved having a good laugh at the expense of one or other of his workmates, the tricks he had pulled in his time. But this started to look sorta serious as his long-time rigbuddy Smithers Van Eckhart fell from the rig. Following his acrid vomit into the slippy-slimy sea far far below.

TWO DAYS EARLIER

In the rig mess hall, Smithers Van Erkhart, Tommy Tool Room and The Fatboy were having a piss up, you know, ginger moonshine fermented in the love bucket of one of those rickety old pleasure droids they shipped out to these spirit-broken colonies, to keep the lads 'appy. Well, everyone knows, you hardly ever get to fuck with these contraptions. It is like rubbing your English Policeman's helmet with a rusting monkey wrench. Maybe that is the point—you don't want your woman-starved employees putting it away night and day.

It was soon understood that the best way to 'utilise' these love droids was to ferment ginger beer in them. And they did a grand job. Made drinking the potent brew quite a thrill too, because of where it was dispensed from, beats those old vodka ice sculptures into a cocked hat, let me tell you. Well, the subject for tonight's philosophical blather was rape.

Specifically, how can you rape one of those Kendra-Xtremes?

Think about it, that's what they did. They would fuck any which way. They even had research going back through fourteen alien civilisations and morph capabilities you could only dream of. They just felt like crap. Raping means against someone's will. Without their permission. But your average love droid was full of permission. All the time, any which way.

The guys guzzled their ginger moonshine from the gaping love hole of Kendra-Xtreme. That wasn't her name, by the way, it was her model. But the guys all called her Kendra-Xtreme, like she was the latest brand of washing soda or toe-cap shiner. She stood there, straddling the gap between two mess hall tables. Kendra-Xtreme never wore anything, what would be the point. Like Maccac monkeys, you could just stop one of the bitches in the hallway between shifts, flip her round round, shove your old chief constable into the cash register and kerching, up would pop the total. Total, as in submission. They never said NO!! never got bored, never phoned the law, never stripped you of your dignity in court, while your shocked family weep and weep, always keen to experiment, you know.

How can you "rape" something that forthcoming? After hours of supping Kendra-Xtreme's ginger brew, the three drunks concocted this phenomenal plan.

They all three engaged in a conversation with the pleasure model as she lay lushus-prone in breeding position.

"Hey, Kendra-X, it's Smithers and Fatboy and the boys. Can we make funny business with you?" Fatboy had rode the hide of Kendra before and almost caved the precious machine-pussyhound in, mainly her torso area.

"You make me soo horny, A number one boys!" she cooed.

"Tell us a story," Smithers said.

Kendra-Xtreme shifted chips doubleplus solid state:

On the Road to Mandalay
Where the flying fishes play
Where the dawn comes out like thunder
Outer China 'crost the bay

She even said it in Kipling mode, thick BBC accent. "What kinda story is that? Spread them there legs, little filly."

"Sure, A number one man! I love, loooove you. All of you!"

"You got a gash, and I got a gasket!", Fatboy said.

"Change that gasket on her." The pubic hair was as fine as Chinese silk spun by a worm on a chinaball tree leaf.

Kendra-Xtreme cooed and moved her lushus-sweet valley thighs, starting to get primed up, the moist circuitry kicked in somewhere deep inside. Her head shook with hair-supermodel sexuality as she brushed her delicate fingers through the blonde hair mane on her sweet little head. Fatboy poured in the electrolyte ginger beer go-juice. It sieved through the gasket above the clit, and went to her neuroneuro funny bouncy bouncy mechanism. Otherwise known as redundant unit #358KJU. That's when Kendra-Xtreme lit up, her eyes wide open and then shut—pur orgasmic synthopleasure, like liquor hitting the lesion on Poe's brain, pure celestial sex joy. A high unlike the cherry high of Martian killspice. Her tits bounced high over land and sea, her skin that of Byronic pleasure-ridden joy, her thatch of nether regions, moist cunt-sweetest cunt there was in the galaxy. So what if it was plastic-methalene-puffpastry bioplasmics—it was sweet pussy. A smell of pherophero musk came and wafted to all the boys. It

was all very romantic, a unique aerosol emission specially formulated
to stimulate each thug's personal thaaang.

Kendra-Xtreme had a perfect memory and at will, or if prompted,
she could replay a verbal breakdown of the more sensual titbits from
each and any session she had ever shared with customer A, B, C or
D . . . This was her device, her way into your love spot, she would
tease out the necessary arousal to fill her love hole to the brim and
have you quivering for more as you emptied into her, so she, meta-
phorically and historically, was filled.

This would turn out to be her great Achilles' heel—her memory.
And the gang knew there was nothing more against her will than a
direct violation of that memory. Well, always the clever one with a
tool hence his name, it was Tommy Tool Room who levered open
her back-skull circuit panel cover. He just pulled the claw hammer
from his back pocket as he threw the old heave-ho into the grunt-
ing sighing Kendra-Xtreme, flipped open the filth smeared cover and
whipped out the memory chip, lickety split.

At first, they all stood there, in their panting sweats, trousers
round their ankles, half erect like three weak salutes, wondering
what to do next. Nobody had ever turned one off before. This was
uncharted territory. For the rest of the off-peak not one of the trio
was allowed to fuck the Kendra-Xtreme. Not one of them was even
allowed to piss into her face or shit on her tongue. Not one of them
was allowed to flip back her perfect little eyelids and rub the head of
his cheesy cock on her perfectly long eyelashes. Not one of them covered her gaping mouth in man batter or took pictures of her gaping
sex all artificially tinted and textured like the skin of an octopus.
She would have let you mind, she looooved you to experiment with
her—that was her function, Goddamit. And in her private mind state,
she had a megalithic portfolio of action she regularly relayed back to
Earth base over the network of ancient radio transmitters. All admis-
sible evidence come the trial.

The fuckdoll weirdness starting to go off Big Time within the
first half hour of Kendra-Xtreme's memory being flipped out. It was
a smell none of them had ever smelt before. Try as they might, they
couldn't place it. It was not of their sex nor species, they surmised. But
after a good few minutes inhaling the not-right musky eye stinger, the
Fatboy leapt onto the steaming carcase and began banging away on

any orifice like he was banging airhostesses in a plummeting Transopter. His back got all rashy and raw and the guys had to pull him off. Tommy Tool Boy tried too. But that was not the end of their troubles and it would take the trio's porn drugged logic a fatal 35 minutes to reinitialise her flipped out memory chip.

In the meantime . . . Kendra-Xtreme warbled in a southern accent: "My, beauty is such a transitory possession. I have always depended upon the kindness of strangers . . ." She tried to smile but began crying a kind of lubricant-ductile. Her face appeared to melt surreally.

Fatboy said, "Oh, we done did it now. The foreman's gonna kick our asses and dock us."

Kendra-Xtreme spoke at 78 revs per second. "Officer, arrest that man! That blackguard! That Highwayman!"

Fatboy chuckled. "She don't know nothing or don't know what the shit she is saying! I wanna squeeze her tits one more time!"

"Shit man, you is a cold-hearted mother! We do stole her mind! Aint that cruelty to a machine pussy?" griefed Tommy Tool Room.

"That dumbassed foreman won't know shit. We'll just tell him I crushed the whore's belly and computer guts when i climbed up on her. Hell, I already kinda did once when I got sloppy seconds off that software cunt!"

The Kendra-Xtreme cried torrents and waterworks of malaise, melancholia, cruelty-given emotion, she was having a built-in body breakdown, where the cpu unit shuts down temporarily to reboot and try and recover from a massive disk failure. And she cried through the whole process. Lakes of pain etched on her face like those canals on Mars; the suffering of Nijinsky in her blinking eyes. Retrograde denouement of beauteous brain fugging. They would just replant her chip in some other synthetic armament and off she'd go—reformatted.

PROLOGUE

It was Smithers, the suicide case, who had concocted the plan of retribution. Sure, they would just send another K-X lickety split, dropping it from geo stationary orbit on its own sleaze-blasting crotchless-

panty jetpack of absolute Bond-movie-ness. But Christ, how he missed his Redhed-Z. That was the name of her model, and she may not have been as sassy, as accommodating, as NearlyReal as your Kendra-X, but she was a traditional pleasure droid. No body morphing, no phero-monic manipulation, no seductions you couldn't break away from. No need to please. Basic but somehow, more . . .

Smithers had this special name for the Redhed-Z that he whispered into her vaguely low-density foam ear, JaneJaneJaneJaneJaneJane. The look in her slightly twisted eyes when they strapped her back into her wrought iron delivery box and shot her up into the atmosphere to the ever-hungry geo-stationary.

He couldn't live without her.

AUTHORS AND ARTISTS

Kim Westwood has had only one thing published before: a totally true Girl's Own Motorcycle story, in *Two Wheels* magazine. Parked as it was between Matho's informative article on Speed Triples and Smithy's hot revs exposé of fat-wheeled mega motor Dukes, it felt like a real coup.

She then wrote a nearly true story about ballroom dancing, which no dance magazine would admit to even having read. It may have been a mistake to combine the chiffon with the Brylcreem like that. Thinking that the term 'speculative' might apply to her, she sent a potentially true story in to a competition and won The Gregor Samsa Prize for Short Speculative Fiction. She is very happy that *Redsine* likes it too.

She lives in a treeful, leafy house in Canberra with her partner and their RSPCA Special dog, Biscuit, and is currently writing several stories, none of which will behave.

Shane M. Brown currently writes from Brisbane, where he lives with his beautiful wife and an only slightly less beautiful cat. "Late Returns" is story number five in a self-imposed fifty short story apprenticeship.

L.H. Maynard & M.P.N. Sims. By the end of 2002 Len Maynard & Mick Sims will have produced 40 books in the genre, as well as having numerous stories published in other people's books. Details can be found at www.maynard-sims.com. Active Horror Writers Association members, their collections, *Shadows At Midnight*, 1979 and

1999, and *Echoes Of Darkness*, 2000, have been followed in 2002 by their third collection, *Incantations*, and the fourth, *Falling Into Heaven* is out in 2003. 2001 saw *Moths*, their novella, available in USA, and in 2002 the novella *The Hidden Language Of Demons* has been published. Also out in 2002 are two collections of their stories, essays and interviews, *The Secret Geography Of Nightmare* and *Selling Dark Miracles*, one introduced by Hugh Lamb and the other by Stephen Jones. A young adult novel, *The Seminar*, is completed. As editors they produce *Darkness Rising* the USA anthology series, and have out in 2002 the retrospective anthology, *Best Of Enigmatic Tales*, and an original anthology, *Cold Touch* (with William Simmons). As publishers they ran Enigmatic Press in the UK, which produced *Enigmatic Tales*, and its sister titles. They co-edited and published *F20* (with David Howe) for The British Fantasy Society. Currently they are putting the finishing touches to a horror novel, *Shelter*, working on a new horror novel, *Stronghold*, progressing a crime novel, *Mere Mortals*, and are planning a novel version of *Demons*.

Richard Robbins. My fiction has been accepted for publication by, or has appeared in, *Happy*, *Virginia Adversaria*, *Algonquin Roundtable Review*, *Snow Monkey*, *Yellow Sticky Notes*, *Leapings Literary Magazine*, *Enigma*, *Barbaric Yawp*, *Samsara*, *Black Petals*, *Futures Magazine*, *Liquid Ohio*, *Penny-A-Liner*, *Raskolnikov's Cellar*, *Heist! Magazine*, *The Armchair Aesthete*, *Trail's End*, *Up Dare?*, *The Nocturnal Lyric*, *Blood Moon Rising*, *Blood Samples*, *No Experience Required* and *Roughneck Review*. My poetry has been published in *Up Dare?*

I was on the Editorial Board of Harvard Yearbook Publications which published the *Harvard Yearbook*, the *Radcliffe Yearbook* and *Cambridge 38*, a magazine.

D.F. Lewis. With around 1,400 published stories between 1986 and 2001, and the special Karl Edward Wagner Award presented to him by the British Fantasy Society in 1998, his published collections include *Only Connect* (written in collaboration with his father), *The Weirdmonger's Tales*, and *The Best of D F Lewis*. He also wrote the novella *Agra Aska*, published by Scorpion Press in 1998. He has now given up writing (except collaborations) but he edits *Nemonymous*, a rare breed of print magazine/anthology in which all fiction is initially published anonymously, inaugurated last November to critical acclaim. Visit the *Nemonymous* website at www.nemonymous.com.

David Mathew was born to the north of London and returned to the general area after working abroad in Cairo and Gdansk. He has sold 300 pieces to magazines, journals and websites, and has recently completed a novel about manipulation, obsession and disease.

Darren Speegle's work has appeared, or is forthcoming, in various publications, including *Chiaroscuro*, *The Dream People*, *5 Trope*, *Wicked Hollow*, *Darkness Rising*, *Horrorfind* and *Underworlds*. Visit his website at www.geocities.com/koobie2stoobies. Darren resides in Germany.

Of **David Alexander**, the Renaissance satirist Francesco Berni has written:

"He walks through Rome dressed like a duke. He takes part in all the wild doings of the lords. He pays his way with insults couched in tricked up words. He talks well, and he knows every libellous anecdote in the city. The Estes and the Gonzagas walk arm in arm with him, and listen to his prattle. He treats them with respect, and is haughty to everyone else. He lives on what they give him. His gifts as a satirist make people afraid of him, and he revels in hearing himself called a cynical, impudent slanderer. All that he needed was a fixed pension. He got one by dedicating to the Pope a second-rate poem."

Forrest Aguirre lives in Madison, Wisconsin with his wife and four children.

He is an inventory analyst in real life, which has nothing to do with his previous life as a graduate student wherein he earned a Master's degree in African History from the University of Wisconsin - Madison. His work has appeared in such venues as *Flesh & Blood*, *Indigenous Fiction*, *The Earwig Flesh Factory*, *The Journal of Experimental Fiction*, and the online version of *Redsine*, among others. He is due to receive an honorable mention in this year's *Year's Best Fantasy and Horror* for his tale "The Universal Language of Silence". "The Butterfly Artist," a chapbook of his short fiction, is to be released in late summer 2002 by Flesh & Blood press. Forrest is managing editor for Ministry of Whimsy press, producers of the *Leviathan* series of anthologies. He is a member of Storyville. Forrest can be reached via email at: chromatic30@hotmail.com.

D. Harlan Wilson's fiction has appeared in a number of American, British and Australian magazines, among them *Doorknobs & BodyPaint, Redsine, Eclectica, Samsara Quarterly, The Café Irreal, The Dream Zone, Fables, Locus Novus, Thunder Sandwich* and *3 A.M. Magazine*. His first full-length book, a collection of forty-four stories called *The Kafka Effekt*, was published in 2001; and his next book, *Inoperative Communities*, another collection of stories, is scheduled to be published at the end of 2002. Wilson holds two M.A. degrees, one in English Literature (University of Massachusetts-Boston), the other in Science Fiction Studies (University of Liverpool). Currently he is working on his Ph.D. in Twentieth Century American Literature and Theory at Michigan State University. (D. Harlan Wilson's official website: www.msu.edu/~dhw/ dharlanwilson/enter.html.)

Stephen A. Vicinanza. I am a full timer writer, living on the Chesapeake Bay, grew up in New York City, have a life long love affair with nature and the supernatural. I have studied science and humanities.

Mark Zirbel lives and writes in Milwaukee, Wisconsin. His fiction has appeared in Webzines such as *Suspect Thoughts* and *Cherry Bleeds*. Most recently, Mark received an honorable mention award in the Eighth Annual Chiaroscuro / Leisure Books Short Story Contest for his story "Seven Souls."

Jane Gwaltney. I'm a Middle-American artist and writer of fiction and poetry with the apparent tendency to blend genres. Recent publication credits include *Dreams and Nightmares, Whispers From the Shattered Forum, The Midnight Gallery,* and MillenniumShift.

Robert Stephenson works in the heart of the Sf and Fantasy industry. Spending all of his time scampering between writing, editing and running his literary agency, www.altair-australia.com. He has had stories appear all over the world in publications like Britain's *Interzone,* Poland's *Nowa Fantasyka,* USA's *Talebones, 1000Delights* and Australia's *Aurealis* and *Orb*. His first novel is now complete and doing the rounds and a second and third are well underway. He is married to Alice, his lovely proof reader and has two beautiful children, Emma 6yrs and Joshua 3yrs. He also thinks it is an absolute pleasure to have a story in the new and wonderful looking *Redsine*. In his own words, "I'm impressed".

Hertzan Chimera (aka Mike Philbin). Nominated for the Pushcart Prize 2001, Mike has been writing as Hertzan Chimera since about 1991 and has collaborated with DF Lewis, Mike Korn, Paul Pinn, Greg Wharton, David C Kopaska-Merkel, David Mathew, Alex Severin, Wrath James White, Christina Sng and Doll Yoko. He is a very active member of the Wordhunger writer's collective.

His novels *Szmonhfu* And *United States* are available through Eraserhead Press. His short story collection (co-written with Wrath James White and Alex Severin) is available from Medium Rare Books.

Check out the 'official' website www.hertzanchimera.com

M. F. Korn has written eleven novels and had over 200 story appearances in magazines worldwide. Currently available are the two paperback collections: *Confessions of a Ghoul and Other Stories* and *Aliens, Minibikes, and Other Staples of Suburbia* and a novel, *Skimming the Gumbo Nuclear*. He resides in Louisiana as a programmer with a degree in Computer Science, and has a daughter, Savannah, five years old. Mike also has a degree in Piano and enjoys playing Rachmaninoff, Gershwin, Chopin and ragtime, and listening to Requiems, Sacred Masses for the Dead.

Caniglia. Born . . . July, 13th 1970 in Omaha, Nebraska USA.(It was Friday the 13th.)

Thoughts . . . There is nothing more pure in life than a canvas waiting to be brought to life by a fury of precision brushstrokes with images of nothing more than concrete irrationality. I believe that as artists, it is up to us to create our own sense of reality. In an age of social and political upheaval, the artist is an anomaly. As creators, we are capable of manipulating the viewer by the stroke of a brush. I paint to live; the canvas is my skin, the paints are my blood, and my brush is the key that unlocks my mind. My artwork may seem traditional in style; nonetheless, it is radical in content, bold and forceful in imagery. I bathe in the reservoir of the poor and oppressed. My statements , like my clear and articulate brush strokes, are sharp, uncompromising, and somber.

Education . . . My formal education in art began at Iowa State

University, where I received my B.F.A. in Drawing, Painting, and Printmaking in 1993. I continued my education at the Maryland Institute College of Art, where I received my M.F.A. Masters in Fine Art in 1995.

Currently . . . My art has really progressed in the last 5 years. I have four major shows lined up in the U.S. and I am currently working out the details for a show in the Netherlands. The shows in the US. will take place in Omaha, Oklahoma City, Chicago, and one in Detroit. My art in books and magazines has also made great strides recently. I illustrated 8 books in 2002 and have had my art featured in magazines as well. I love bringing stories to life. Creating is all I know. It is so incredible to extract a vision from my mind and share it with the reader as there storyteller. Some of the recent books that feature my art on covers and interiors are Douglas Clegg's *Breeder* and *The Machinery of Night*. Tim Lebbon's *White and Other Tales of Ruin* and Edward Lee's *Dark Addictions*.

Simon Duric. Born Simon John Duric in 1978 on 3rd of November in little village in Derbyshire, I now live in Nottingham working as a Bar Manager as well as studying Graphic Design. Grew up on an unhealthy diet of Ray Harryhausen classics like 'Jason and the Argonauts' before progresssing onto the likes of 'Alien' and 'The Terminator'. After leaving Art College I spent 3 years in the widerness doing shit jobs like warehouse work, driving forklift trucks, working in t shops, building sites, flyering, painting and decorating. A 6 month stint at the beginning of 2001 bumming in Spain allowed me to develop my style so I came back and got my first work for *The Third Alternative*. I've also worked for *Dreamzone, Kimota, Legends, Roadworks, Hidden Corners, Mosquito, Prime,* and *Redsine*. My dream is to be like Giger and Mckean and work on books, comics, CD's, Computer games and films. I do most of my work in Pencil Crayons but also use Inks and Pen and am currently branching into digital artwork and photography. My creative influences and inspirations come from Dave Mckean, HR Giger, Rick Berry, Alessandro Bavari, David Ho, Mike Bohatch, Joachim Luetke, Carravaggio, Hieronymous Bosch, Joel peter Witkin, David Fincher, Steven Spielberg, James Cameron, Michael Marshall Smith, Brian Lumley, Anne Rice, Clive Barker, Dean Koontz, Jimi Hendrix, Red Hot Chilli Peppers, The Prodigy and all the freaks who walk into my bar night after night! [simonduric@hotmail.com]

LEVIATHAN 3

Libri quosdam ad scientiam, alios ad insaniam deduxere

Edited by Forrest Aguirre & Jeff VanderMeer

Leviathan Three is the third volume in the World Fantasy Award and British Fantasy Award finalist Ministry of Whimsy's Leviathan series. Twenty-seven beautifully surreal stories, informed by the exotic, yet infused with clear, controlled prose, give even the most voracious reader of the sublime an abundant feast of words and images. The tales are, by turns, experimental, traditional, uplifting, and mischievous. From the early decadent works of Gautier and Gourmont to experimental fictions by such established writers as Rikki Ducornet, Brian Evenson, Carol Emshwiller, and Michael Moorcock, to fresh perspectives from up-and-coming writers James Bassett, Brendan Connell, and Michael Cisco, Leviathan 3 fullfills the expectations created by prior volumes, while further exploring the expanse of convulsive beauty. Zoran Zivkovic's "Library" story suite, or short novel, provides the impetus and frame for the anthology, as each Library story is followed by a series of thematically similar selections. Zivkovic, a highly-respected Yugoslavian writer, has reached new heights of metafiction, intellectual play, and emotional resonance with these stories about books.

"Perhaps the outstanding original anthology of 2002 . . . what the anthology promises it delivers, and story after story is intriguing reading." —**Locus**

Praise for previous volumes in the Leviathan series:

"A big, handsome devil . . . just about everything wins reader confidence early and then maintains it with intelligent development" —**Literary Magazine Review**

" . . . One of the best collections of quality fiction at any level that I've seen in years."
—**Tangent**

ISBN: 1-894815-42-4

Price: $21.95

THE MINISTRY OF WHIMSY PRESS
World Fantasy Award & British Fantasy Award Finalist
Publisher of Stepan Chapman's Philip K. Dick Award-winning The Troika

LEVIATHAN #3, edited by Forrest Aguirre & Jeff VanderMeer

"Decadent fantasy has rarely had this attractive and substantial a vehicle." —**Nick Gevers, Locus**

"The variety and ambition of this compilation mandates that lovers of speculative fiction consider it for their own self-defined libraries." —**Publisher's Weekly**

"Good and clever enough to send readers and librarians scurrying to find its predecessors." —**Ray Olsen, Booklist**

The third volume in the highly-acclaimed Leviathan series, showcasing beautifully dark surreal work by such authors as Michael Moorcock, Rikki Ducornet, Stepan Chapman, Brian Stableford and Zoran Zivkovic. Trade paperback. 484 pages. Full color cover by Dawn Andrews. ISBN 1-894815-42-4. $21.95 plus shipping.

LEVIATHAN #2, edited by Jeff VanderMeer & Rose Secrest

"A big, handsome devil…just about everything wins reader confidence early and then maintains it with intelligent development. Too bad there isn't an issue out every month." - *Literary Magazine Review*

"…a refreshing change from the bland literalness of many genre stories…the prose style is crystalline and condensed, poetic…" - *Locus*

The British Fantasy Award-finalist novellas volume, with an essay-introduction by *Interzone* editor David Pringle. Featuring work by Stepan Chapman, Richard Calder, L. Timmel Duchamp, Rhys Hughes. Trade paperback. 192 pages. Duotone cover by Scott Eagle. ISBN 1-8904-6403-1. $10.99 plus shipping.

www.ministryofwhimsy.com